C000184383

THE FASCINATION
OF EVIL

FLORIAN ZELLER

THE FASCINATION
OF EVIL

Translated from the French
by Sue Dyson

PUSHKIN PRESS
LONDON

English translation © Sue Dyson & Pushkin Press

First published in French as
La Fascination du pire © Flammarion 2004

This edition first published in 2006 by
Pushkin Press
12 Chester Terrace
London N1 4ND

British Library Cataloguing in Publication Data:
A catalogue record for this book is available
from the British Library

ISBN (13) 978 1 901285 65 9
ISBN (10) 1 901285 65 0

All rights reserved. No part of this publication may be
reproduced, stored in a retrieval system or transmitted in
any form or by any means, electronic, mechanical,
photocopying, recording or otherwise,
without prior permission in writing from
Pushkin Press

Cover: *Street in Old Cairo* circa 1900 Robert L Bracklow
© Photo Collection Alexander Alland Sr & Corbis

Frontispiece: Florian Zeller 2004
courtesy of Flammarion

Set in Monotype Baskerville
and printed in Jordan
by National Press

*Ouvrage publié avec le concours du
Ministère Français chargé de la culture—Centre national du Livre*

WARNING

*This book is fiction: the majority of what is said in
it is not true; the rest, by definition, isn't either.*

THE FASCINATION
OF EVIL

1

TAKING THE PLANE

A S THE ALARM CLOCK RANG, I wished I'd never agreed to this trip. It was still dark, and I had hardly slept at all. I should have gone to bed earlier the previous evening, I told myself. But that wasn't my style. And besides, I could always sleep on the plane.

I got up to make myself some coffee. I looked out of the kitchen window. It was five am, but Paris hadn't woken up yet. Nor had Jeanne. Once I was dressed, I went and watched her sleeping. I don't know why, but I've always found her at her most beautiful in the morning, her body like a refuge against the dawn's cold. I wrote her a note, telling her I was going to miss her. Sometimes, a week is a very long time. And besides, I was afraid I'd never see her again. It's ridiculous, I agree, but that's how it was: since the death of my parents, I could no longer ignore the fact that anything could happen at any moment. I would even say that, in a certain way, I was constantly on the lookout for my own death. By telling her I would miss her, it seems to me that I was in reality trying to say farewell to her. In fact I was a little upset, but in an excessive and unpleasant way. It hadn't done me any favours, waking up so early. After all, it was only a trip lasting a few days. I tore up the note and threw it into the bin, then closed my suitcase.

The French Embassy in Egypt had invited me to Cairo to give a talk as part of a sort of book fair. On the telephone, the cultural attaché had informed me that Martin Millet would be making the journey with me. (Millet was a quite famous Swiss author, one of whose books I had read a year before: I vaguely recalled a succession of violent, sometimes monstrous fantasies, whose ambition was to describe a market society's sexual misery and in passing, I think, his own.) I received my plane ticket in the post, along with my instructions. In the event, my job was to talk a little on the theme of the 'new French Romantic generation' and, the rest of the time, to take advantage of my stay. In the taxi taking me to Roissy, I told myself that apart from this nocturnal awakening, the whole thing promised to be rather pleasant, and that I must lose this habit of always feeling sorry for myself when I woke up.

A few days earlier, an Egyptian aeroplane had gone down in the Red Sea. It had taken off from Sharm el-Sheikh; all the passengers had perished in the catastrophe. For the most part they were French and were returning home after a week's holiday. The precise reasons for this accident were still not yet known. At first, thoughts had turned to an attack. Then the two black boxes had been retrieved, with the aid of robots able to work at depths in excess of one thousand metres. According to what I'd read the previous day, the recordings ruled out the terrorist hypothesis. So it must have been a 'classic accident'; this was a real relief to (almost) everybody.

In a gesture of solidarity the imam of the mosque, Sheikh Ibrahim al-Saleh, had declared that this tragedy "had not only affected the families of the victims, but all Egyptians". It is true that it didn't suit them much either. This type of accident generally brings about a slump in tourism, and Egypt—which had been in economic crisis for several years—could really do without that. All the more so, since Sharm el-Sheikh is a seaside resort greatly prized by westerners. This is borne out by the proliferation of modern hotels, casinos, tourist villages and shopping centres that have turned the town, with its neon signs, into a sort of Las Vegas of the East.

Travel agencies generally offer two types of holiday in Egypt. The first (which all the accident victims had opted for) takes place on the shores of the Red Sea. *The Ras Mohammed reserve offers a diving site that ranks among the seven most beautiful in the world: the slopes of Shark Reef.* The interest of this trip can be pretty much summed up as that: watching a multitude of multi-coloured tropical fish. The second is an itinerary within the "Egypt of the Pharaohs"; generally, it consists of a Nile cruise. In a period of ten days or so, the tourist visits Cairo (for its museum and its pyramids), Luxor (for its different temples and the Valley of the Kings) and finally Aswan (for its famous dam and the temple at Abu Simbel) … This second formula enjoyed enormous success until one morning in November 1997, when a group of Islamic terrorists massacred all the tourists in the Temple of Hatshepsut, at Luxor—a magnificent spot, incidentally.

Over the previous few years, I had travelled quite a lot in Muslim countries, notably in the Middle East. My encounter with a Jordanian woman had given me a taste for the region. On the other hand, I had only visited Egypt once. It was in 1998, with my parents. Like a lot of tourists, we had taken advantage of the very favourable prices offered by the travel agencies after the attacks at Luxor. At that time, since demand had fallen dramatically, you could easily take a cruise on the Nile for less than two thousand francs. What's more, by dropping prices drastically in this way, the country managed little by little to recover from the consequences of the massacre. But in order to offer these kinds of prices, I told myself that morning as I arrived at Roissy, there had to be savings made somewhere, in other words a cut in variable costs, among them not only the quality of service, but security. Now, everything suggested that the Sharm el-Sheikh accident had been due to technical failure, and more precisely to an inability to control the plane. In other words, this air disaster was an indirect consequence of the Islamic killings. In this respect, the imam at the mosque was indeed right: this tragedy didn't just affect the families of the victims.

It was still dark when the taxi dropped me off at the airport. I told myself that it wasn't very clever to dwell on all this just before getting on an aeroplane. I was just frightening myself for no good reason. It was better to think about positive things. But which ones? One accident never happens immediately after another, it's a well-known fact. In this respect, it was the ideal moment to leave for Egypt. Basically, nothing could happen to me. That's what I told myself for reassurance.

I went off to buy a few newspapers before heading for the check-in desk. I'd been asked to arrive two hours early. Since September 11th, the checks had become interminable. Of course I knew that Egypt was a predominantly Muslim country, but I was nonetheless surprised to find that I was almost the only person in the queue not wearing a djellaba. I swallowed hard. All the women were veiled. In this day and age it's regrettable, djellabas, veils and aeroplanes give you funny ideas.

Suddenly I felt a hand on my shoulder. I started. I turned around: it was Martin Millet. I had seen a photo of him, so I had already noted the slightly odd shape of his face, his very clear resemblance to a pet animal that's been run over, but I had imagined him as being stronger and taller. He was aged about thirty. We shook hands. He seemed quite pleased to be there. All smiles. This was the first time he'd been to Egypt. And undoubtedly the last. But he didn't know that yet.

"So," he asked with an enthusiasm that seemed exaggerated to me, "have you been there before?"

"Once, yes."

"And?"

In reality, I entirely associated this country with my parents, since it was with them I'd gone there—our last trip before their accident. But I had promised myself I would be strong and not lapse into melancholy: five years had already passed, and I couldn't keep revisiting their deaths for ever. I chose to say that I didn't remember the precise details—a fact which wasn't entirely untrue.

"It's rather a pity we can't visit the south. People tell me Luxor's the place you really have to see … "

It's true that with the planned talks, it was difficult to see us leaving Cairo. Or perhaps just for a day. I had been told that the library at Alexandria, for example, was a 'must see'. But nothing makes one less inclined to go and see something than when that thing is a 'must see'. Things that you 'must see' are generally of only limited interest. By way of example, in Paris the Arc de Triomphe is a 'must see'.

"Yeah," I replied then, voicing my thoughts …

Basically, staying in Cairo didn't bother me. For me, it's perhaps the best way to understand a country: walking through the capital city with no specific goal. As I recalled, Cairo was a gigantic city, exhausting and dusty, but which gave off a rather fantastic energy. I had initially planned to go to the Orthodox monastery of Saint Catherine, in Sinai, but after consulting a map, I gave up the idea. To do the return trip in a day, I would have had to take an internal flight with a dodgy company. And since Sharm el-Sheikh, I didn't really fancy that. After all, I'd be just as well off in the hotel swimming pool in Cairo.

It took me a while to understand why the majority of the passengers didn't look like Egyptians: the plane first made a stop in Cairo, as it did once every week, before setting off again for Jeddah, in Saudi Arabia. "It's just our luck," Martin said. All these folk were in reality pilgrims, heading for Mecca. Then I remembered that each year dozens, sometimes hundreds of them died, trampled to death in the enlightened crowd. But travelling by plane under these conditions is an interesting experience: for example, it enables you with hindsight to appreciate the serenity of your daily life.

Martin was sitting on my right. He was already trying to work the little screen set into the back of the seat in front. To my left, a man was complaining to an air hostess because his wife, who was veiled from head to foot, was not sitting on his right (that is to say, in my seat); he said that he would not tolerate having a man sitting next to her. There was something rather contradictory about taking a plane and then raging against the possibility of having someone next to you. They should have suggested he buy a private plane. This man had very beautiful eyes. Long lashes that gave him a delicate, even feminine air. What did he find so fearsome? Did he really doubt his power over her to that extent? The hostess didn't look surprised by his reaction. She was a professional. She said that she understood, even though—I am convinced—she didn't understand any better than I did. "We have to understand," her eyes seemed to be trying to tell me, "it's cultural. He would see it as an insult if a guy was seated next to his wife … "

"An insult to what?" I could have asked (but I had no desire to complicate the situation).

"To her modesty," would have been the reply.

"And the woman in question would have to be a potential object of desire," Martin then whispered in my ear. Which was manifestly not the case: she looked rather like a plump, indistinct mass. You could tell that even through her veil. The man who sat next to her, he assured me, wouldn't even have looked at her. But fine, if it was cultural ... So everyone had to change places so that modesty could be preserved. And finally the plane could take off.

Martin fell asleep quite quickly. As for me, a series of suspicious noises kept me on edge. I had Sharm el-Sheikh in my head, as well as those words by Cyrano about his nose: "It's like the Red Sea when it bleeds!" To change my thoughts, I read the newspapers I'd bought at the airport. *Libération* led on Alain Juppé's conviction. An eighteen-month suspended sentence, ten years' ineligibility, and all this for involvement in secret financial deals. Clearly this was the important information of the day. The rest was a little more conventional: some guy had got himself blown up in Iraq, Israel had retaliated in Bethlehem and Sharon declared that the 'security cordon' was more necessary than ever ... By a sort of irony, the *Figaro Magazine*'s cover featured *The strange Tariq Ramadan*. In the last few weeks, he had been seen a great deal during the media chaos provoked by the law on secularism. Endowed with an undeniable seductive power, this populist extremist's declared ambition was to convert Europe to Islam. Reading this article, I learned that he was the grandson of the founder of the Muslim Brothers, an organisation actually created in Egypt, and that it could justly be regarded as the ideological cradle of modern Islamism. Then I remembered a recent broadcast, during which Ramadan had attempted to justify the wearing of the veil by talking about this famous 'modesty'. A philosopher facing him had calmly replied: "In that case, why don't men wear the veil? Is a woman's face more immodest than a man's?"

I put down the papers. I closed my eyes for a moment, but couldn't get to sleep. For a while now, I'd been tortured by interminable periods of sleeplessness, and I couldn't seem to recover. An air hostess came down the aisle to offer us cool drinks. She spoke loudly, in an unpleasant voice, and Martin woke up. He rubbed his face, as if he had slept for three thousand nights on the trot. I ordered an apple juice.

"I can't stand women with loud voices," he grumbled once she had moved away.

The man on my left certainly wasn't going to contradict him.

"Yes, but she's pretty."

Martin turned round.

"Yeah. Not bad. Despite the uniform."

"Actually, I generally find air hostesses rather exciting, with their uniforms."

"You think so?"

I then thought back to an interview the singer Prince had given in a women's magazine: they'd asked him what his favourite dish was, and he'd replied: air hostesses. I don't know why, but that stuck with me, and I've never forgotten that answer, to the point that I think of it every time I get on a plane. Are they really girls of easy virtue? It's an important question. To this was added what I'd been told about the gigantic orgies that took place during stopovers among the members of the crew. I had no idea if it was a myth, but each time a steward passed me in the corridor, I couldn't help saying to myself: you sly devil, you're going to have yourself a good time ... And similarly, each time I encountered a hostess, I had the definite feeling that I was dealing with a whore ...

"Do you live with anyone?" I asked him.

"Yeah ... It's kind of complicated."

"It's always complicated."

"I don't doubt it."

"She's not an air hostess, is she?"

He gave me a sad smile and didn't answer. I felt a bit bloody stupid. Then, after a moment's silence, he explained to me that he no longer believed in the notion of the 'couple'. As he saw it, it was a structure for dominating the other person, built from lies, and one which no longer had any place. He preferred the notion of a 'favourite person', which allowed one more freedom and which was more honest. He frowned as he explained this to me, as if it were a very personal concept, whereas the dissolution of the married couple is on the contrary one of the West's most serious tendencies.

Two broad aisles ran the length of the Boeing, separating three rows of seats; each passenger had a little screen, connected to a programme of films, games and music. We had been talking for almost an hour. He explained to me that he had left Switzerland five years previously and settled in Paris. Deep down, I was quite pleased not to be going on my own. And Martin seemed rather interesting. Since the start, he had had Flaubert's *Correspondence* on his knees—one of my favourite books. I told him that it was strange to be setting off for Egypt with this big book and, as I said this, I remembered that there were a few letters regarding his journey to the East, notably a few letters written in Egypt. He confirmed this enthusiastically. It was precisely because of these letters that he had brought the whole volume. He wanted to read them in their original setting.

"The really funny thing," he continued, "is that when he arrives in Cairo, his first letters are to his mother. He describes what he sees to her, but in reality he's describing what she would like to see. It's just like a postcard. Wait, I'll find the bit for you … "

He opened his annotated collection and searched through it for a moment, his mouth open. Then he read out loud:

"*At sunset, the Sphinx and the three Pyramids, which were pink all over, seemed drowned in light; the old monster gazed at us, terrifying and motionless. I shall never forget that singular impression. We slept there for three nights, at the foot of those old women the Pyramids, and frankly it's grand.*"

"And?"

"And, the funny thing is, at the same time he's writing to his friends, and recounting his tours of the bordellos … You'll see … There!

Now, my dear sir, we are in a land where the women are naked, and one might say with the poet 'naked as one's hand', for their only clothing consists of rings. I've fucked girls from Nubia who had necklaces of gold piastres that reached down to their thighs, and who wore belts of coloured beads on their black bellies."

"He certainly isn't going to tell his mother that … When does it date from?"

"It's a letter from … 1849."

"Yes, because today, you can't really say that women are naked in that country … It would be rather the opposite, if I've understood correctly."

"For my part, I think it's still like that. We'll see, but it wouldn't surprise me if they sleep around … The Orientals are a lot more sensual than we are. Wait! A bit further on …
*In the doorways, women standing, or seated on mats. The negresses had sky-blue dresses, others were yellow, white, red—loose garments that float on the hot wind … *"

Suddenly he stopped. A section of the passengers had stood up as one. They were probably not all going to the toilet at the same moment. This was something else. Martin and I looked at each other, and I think we thought the same thing. But it wasn't that. The pilgrims calmly settled themselves in the aisles, got down on the floor and started to pray. It was time; the plane had suddenly been transformed into a mosque. Quite openly. I couldn't get over it. It was an incredible sight. And in fact, rather unpleasant. You couldn't walk in the aisles any more. Some of them were imploring so loudly that you could hardly hear yourself speak.

"Suddenly you feel alone, don't you?"

But Martin didn't answer me: he was listening to some music; I looked for the headphones that had been handed out to us, and did the same. Shortly afterwards, while they were still prostrating themselves, the plane crossed an area of turbulence, and the chief cabin steward asked us to go back to our seats. I saw an ironic smile on Martin's face. The majority of the believers refused to hear a thing, for a prayer cannot be interrupted, and they stayed in the aisles, declaiming their verses from the Koran, taking no account of what they'd just been asked to do; they preferred prayer to safety, and that was that.

I wondered what would happen if the turbulence became increasingly severe. Would they hold out until they were knocked over on top of one another? The plane started to move in all directions. I felt increasingly ill at ease. According to the screen in front of me, we were flying over Corsica. Really? I checked that my safety belt was done up securely. What use are safety belts in a crashing plane? That is also an important question. My hands were moist. I was still thinking about Sharm el-Sheikh. From what I understood, the accident had lasted around three minutes, which is a horribly long time. The plane had gone down in free fall. What happens then? People must howl, vomit, throw themselves at each other. A vision of horror.

To reassure myself, I asked Martin if, in a general way, he was afraid in planes. I assumed a detached tone of voice so that this question didn't sound like an admission. Doubtless I was hoping that he would say yes, rather piteously; then I could have assured him that we were in no danger and that it was pointless worrying about a bit of simple turbulence. But, with an annoying assurance, he explained that he had no fear of dying, here or elsewhere.

"I'm increasingly fatalistic, you see. If it's meant to happen, it will happen. That's that."

"That must make things easier for you … "

"That's all my life means to me. And in any case, if there was a problem here, in the middle of the Mediterranean, what could you do? Not much, eh?"

Then, in an almost jovial tone of voice, he told me an impossible story; I think it was intended to clarify his vision of fate.

"The story takes place in New York, on September 11th 2001," he told me, with a slightly perverse jubilation.

"Yes, I've heard about that … "

"No, this is a story within a story … A guy is working in a communications agency whose offices are in one of the two towers, at the precise spot that the plane has bumped into … "

(I wanted to interrupt; I found the use of the verb 'to bump' bizarre. From what I'd seen, the planes had done more than simply 'bump' into the towers, but fine, perhaps it was a Swiss expression.)

"Needless to say all those who were working in these offices are dead. Now, the previous day, this guy's boss falls ill and asks him to take his place, going to visit clients in Washington. Do you realise? The guy's on the point of death, he's done for, and in the end, this saves his life … "

"So what," I said, simulating indifference.

"Wait, that's not the end … the plane he takes that morning is precisely the one that bumps into one of the towers!"

"No!"

"Yes. You see, he couldn't escape his destiny."

In the end I pretended to be asleep: the silence was more reassuring than Martin's anecdotes. By closing my eyes, I almost managed to forget that I was in a plane. Then I thought back to a story someone had told me. For their honeymoon, my uncle and aunt had actually gone to Egypt. At the foot of one of the pyramids, a guy had suggested they take a camel ride, they'd agreed, and the moment my aunt climbed onto the animal, the stranger set off at a gallop, as if he wanted to abduct her, but the animal stopped in its tracks a few yards further on, a whim, and when my uncle caught up with them, he fought this bogus camel-driver. This story then made me think of another anecdote, somewhat similar, but more tragic. A young couple have just arrived in Brazil, again for their honeymoon. They are in a taxi; the driver holds out a letter to the young man and asks him if he'd mind placing it in the letter-box ten metres from the car door. He agrees, calmly gets out of the vehicle, turns round and sees to his terror that the car is no longer there, his fiancée has been abducted, he will never find her again … Then I thought about Jeanne, of waking up, of that idiotic feeling I'd had of perhaps never seeing her again. Turning round, and realising that the car is no longer there.

About ten years after that trip to Egypt, my uncle and aunt got divorced in a way that was as second-rate as it was banal: insulting each other, threatening each other, and attacking each other with petty-minded lawsuits. That is how love stories end today, you know. And the idea of being able to summarise the whole of the other sex in a single person raises a gentle smile: we know now that the freedom of action and exacerbation of desires that characterise the modern era easily overcome innocence and the capacity for illusions. We must now agree that a couple has no chance at all of not breaking up one day. It's a reality that one can ignore. But sometimes I say to myself, with fear in my belly, that I myself could be that camel-driver, I could be that taxi-driver.

When I opened my eyes, the plane had already begun its descent. It was almost noon. I was in a hurry to get there now. We had nothing planned for the day, and that was how I liked it. Martin was reading a guide to Egypt. I asked him if he had found anything interesting.

"It's not bad for someone who knows nothing about it, like me. For example, they say that our hotel is the best in Cairo … "

"Which hotel are we in?"

"The Marriott. There's a bar where you can smoke the finest *chicha*, apparently. And look what they say here about the bar at the casino … *A place where you can meet people if you're disposed to pay* … "

Martin was looking at me, absolutely enchanted.

"You see, I was right: Flaubert doesn't date as quickly as all that! Literature is immortal, and we're soon going to touch down in the land of 'naked women'!"

At that same moment, the plane banked towards the Nile Delta.

2

THE EGYPTIAN NIGHT

THE REPRESENTATIVE OF THE EMBASSY came to fetch us from the airport. Jérémie was under thirty and looked a little like Brazza, that late-nineteenth-century adventurer who had discovered the Congo, and whose portrait I had seen a few weeks previously: straight nose, short beard and a rather intriguing facial paradox—the exact coexistence of a look that said he came from a good family, and a preoccupation that I would classify as more or less romantic. He shook our hands most insistently, and I told myself that he must be bored in this country if he was so happy to see us get off the plane.

An embassy car was waiting for us. In Arabic, Jérémie asked the driver to take us to our hotel, which was a way of showing us that he knew the language well. Incidentally, that was my first question: how long had he been speaking Arabic? Jérémie had arrived in Cairo a year and a half earlier. His posting was supposed to last two years, which meant that he still had six months to go. His job at the Embassy was to promote French culture by regularly organising events and inviting artists. "Cairo intellectuals often speak French. Not all of them, but there's a real tradition and … "

While he was speaking, I wondered what could drive a guy of our age to come and work at the end of the world like this; I didn't think I could do it. I was too attached to Europe.

"What about girls?" Martin went straight to the point.

Jérémie looked uncomfortable and smiled in a complicated way.

"What do you mean, girls?"

"I don't know … I'm not familiar with the situation … Can a Westerner pick up an Egyptian girl, for example?"

"It's very difficult. Here, as a general rule, girls do not sleep around. Islam is very strict about it. But there is a little of everything in Egypt … I mean, there aren't only veiled women, even if they are on the increase."

"But what about you, for example? In your year and a half here, have you been able to meet girls or is it really a lost cause?"

"It's a lost cause, I think … But I must say I'm mostly interested in the girls at the Embassy … "

"French girls?"

"Yes."

During the drive, Jérémie explained the arrangements for our stay. He also handed us a programme detailing everything we were supposed to do during these few days. Contrary to what I had hoped, we weren't going to have much free time. In addition to the talks, a series of lunches and dinners had been organised. A few visits were also planned:

"Tomorrow morning, if you want, we've booked a guide to accompany you to the Cairo Museum … "

"That's nice … "

"Monsieur Cotté will also be with you … "

"The politician?"

"Yes. He's here for a few days. I think he's writing a book about Alexandria … "

Through the window, we received a gradual introduction to the outskirts of Cairo. Rows of palm trees lined the road; there was no doubt about it, we were a long way from Paris.

I had often seen Monsieur Cotté taking part in various political debates on TV. He had 'important' responsibilities within the UMP. In several respects, he was the perfect embodiment of everything that disgusted me about politics: ignorance, pretentiousness and studied optimism. But I wasn't surprised to learn that he was writing a book. For several years now, politicians have all been writing their books (or more exactly, having them written by someone else) to regain a little of the prestige they lose every day in their attempts to seduce morons. It's the most tiresome aspect of an opinion-based democracy: politicians on the right or the left are obliged to try and be smart, on some TV panel or other, to demonstrate that they are basically really nice guys and that people would be wrong not to vote for them. That's what we've come to. So not surprisingly, if they want to avoid being completely discredited, it's best to make people believe they're still interested in something other than their own careers; so they have a little book written for them, they sign it with impunity, cast off their neckties, and go back to the TV panels to try and sell themselves one more time—through force of circumstances, politicians have simply become prostitutes who no longer give pleasure to anyone and who sell off their little tricks at bargain basement prices.

"Have you been to see the library at Alexandria?" I asked Jérémie.

"Yes, of course."

"So what's it like?"

"It's really beautiful and historically quite important. Unfortunately, you won't have time to go there ... "

We were already entering the centre of Cairo. I vaguely recognised these streets I had walked along with my parents. I made an effort not to think of that again. The traffic was so dense that we scarcely dared to open the car windows. The din of the city. Its pollution.

"It's beautiful!" exclaimed Martin.

"It's Cairo: as unbearable as it is magnificent ... "

The Marriott hotel stood on the banks of the Nile. Jérémie lived in an apartment in a different district, but he wanted to accompany us to make sure that we were properly settled in. He handed us both an envelope containing our daily expenses.

"This is to cover what you spend during your stay ... "

It was quite a large sum, amounting to around eighty euros per day. He left us in the lobby, after sorting out the administrative details, and arranged to meet us at the same place early in the evening to go to dinner.

"He seems quite a nice guy, that Jérémie," commented Martin in the lift.

"Yeah."

"Right ... We'll rest for a while and then we'll make a move?"

"Why not."

"We can go and have some *chicha* before we meet up with Jérémie. What do you reckon? In the hotel bar, for example ... "

"With the 'naked women', you mean?"

"Exactly."

"You know, when you have an idea you just won't let go of it ... "

"Quite the opposite," he answered very seriously. "It's the idea that won't let go of me."

Our rooms were on the same floor. I took a shower, then—with a towel around my waist—went out onto the balcony to smoke a cigarette. I had barely opened the sliding glass door when the sublime sound of the city entered my room: hellish cries, engine noise, incessant car horns mingling with the distant call to prayer. In front of me loomed the Cairo Tower, erected in memory of a victory over Israel. I stayed for quite a while gazing upon the eastern city from the seventh floor of the hotel and, without any real reason, I told myself that I felt good—if you can call it 'feeling good', that state of relaxed consciousness which enables you to forget what you've already experienced, and the things you won't fail to relive all over again.

And yet, at the very heart of this oblivion a memory came back to me: a memory of Brittany, of the attic which had been turned into a bedroom for me. I used to spend hours on end there, reading. From the small window, you could see the horizon and in a way it was like being on this hotel balcony, outside the world, but with its hubbub just reaching up as far as me. Yes, in the distance you could see the sea and the strip of gulf, curved round like an arena. And I entertained myself by pinpointing a geometric centre to this perfect curve of sand, towards which a solemn and determined bullfighter was advancing. With a gesture reminiscent of a sacrificial priest, he easily freed life from its tension and liberated ten thousand hearts in one fell swoop. Mine included.

Someone knocked at my door. I went to open it. They'd brought up my suitcase. Then I switched on the TV to see what the local stations were like. There was nothing very interesting on. Not at this time of day, at any rate. I saw that a small parcel had been placed on my bedside locker. I opened it. It was a copy of the Koran, donated by the organisers of the book fair. I thought this was a good idea; I hadn't leafed through it for a long time. I was going to do so, but I think I fell asleep almost immediately.

It was Martin who woke me up by knocking at my door. It was already dark. I stumbled across to open up.

"It's almost eight o'clock. Aren't you ready?"

"Yes I am," I replied, realising that I still had my towel around my waist. "Well, almost."

"I'll wait for you downstairs if you like. In the lobby."

"OK. I'll be right down."

I got dressed in haste. I still felt sleepy, but fine. As I understood it, we were supposed to be having dinner with some friends of Jérémie's in a restaurant in the souk. I put part of my expenses money in the safe, and pulled the door of my room closed behind me.

Martin was sitting in the entrance hall, looking dreamy. He was smoking a cigarette and gazing at a group of veiled young girls, sitting a little further off:

"They really are bizarre, those girls! They never stop making eyes, have you noticed?"

"No. What time are we meeting Jérémie?"

"In an hour. As regards the *chicha*, from what I've read everything happens in the garden … "

He stood up without taking his eyes off the neighbouring table. He seemed really unsettled. I suggested we make a move …

"The funny thing," he went on, "is that I find it rather erotic, a woman with a veil … "

"Oh, really?"

"I mean, if you forget about what it signifies."

" … "

"Don't you find the same?"

I didn't. At first sight, the hotel's clientele was essentially international, but less western than I'd been expecting. They were predominantly Saudis who came here in groups to spend holidays a long way from their own country. I found out later that they were absolutely detested by the local population. "They're big fat pigs," I was told by Lamia, a girl from the Embassy whom I would meet the following day. "At home in Saudi Arabia, they're total extremists! But as soon as they get some distance away, to Morocco, Thailand or Egypt, they're the worst kind of debauchees, and they do precisely the things they condemn! They're rich and the way they flash their money around is obscene! There's a host of girls who flock around those guys, you just can't imagine. It's disgustingly hypocritical!"

As I saw it, the unveiled girls were there especially for them, and not for the western tourists, with all due respect to Martin. Anyway, as he'd said: we'd see.

The hotel's courtyard garden was very strongly scented and quite pleasant, especially at this time of year when the heat was not too unbearable. We crossed it, with the swimming pool on our left.

"There it is!" Martin told me, pointing to the Egyptian Night, an open-air café. There was practically nobody there. We sat at a table and ordered two *chichas*. Not too far away from us, a girl was waiting at a table all on her own and consulting her mobile.

"You see her, for example? She's a whore … "

His obsession was starting to make me smile. I wondered to what degree he kept returning to this subject in order to make fun of himself.

"She's not bad, is she?"

"Why do you say she's a whore?"

"It's obvious! Listen, what would a girl like her be doing there, all alone, on a café terrace, in the garden of a big hotel?"

"I don't know, she might just be drinking a cup of mint tea … "

"No! She's a whore, cut off my hand if she's not!"

She had spotted us. She was even directing ambiguous smiles at Martin. I sensed that he was having difficulty keeping still. A waiter brought us apple-scented *chichas*. I hadn't smoked for several years; as for Martin, he'd never smoked in his life. In general, people who don't know think it's like an opium pipe, and the name *chicha* is immediately associated with that of hashish. I remembered one time when I had smoked with my mother. It must have been a few streets away, in a souk café, a good five years ago now. My brother was there too. She was laughing all by herself, as if her head was spinning—but it's only tobacco. I closed my eyes, and I saw her smile again, full of tenderness. That very special way she had of smiling. And then I breathed in the thick smoke, and it seemed to me that I was only doing so in order to still a profound pain that was trying to well up inside me.

"Mm … nice!" he commented.

"Very," I replied, but I was talking about the *chicha*.

"I think the girls in these countries really have something, you know."

At the same moment, an Arab came and sat at the table where Martin's whore was sitting—for, in his mind at any rate, she was already his. The situation was in danger of becoming farcical. We observed them in silence. Then the man stood up. A moment later, the girl also left the Egyptian Night. Martin seemed furious.

"Calm down, we've only just arrived … "

"Yes, but she was a bit of all right, wasn't she?"

"Frankly, she was very average."

Next, two girls entered and sat down at a table twenty or so metres from us; Martin regained hope. He remained silent for five whole minutes, completely fixated on these two girls. The waiters must have thought we were utterly ridiculous. I saw him regularly direct little smiles at the girls to try and charm them, although on the face of it they had no need of charming. I wondered what kind of life he led in Paris. He must be on his own, despite what he'd told me. Alone and sad—like the majority of people, in fact.

"I think I'm going to go for it," he told me finally, with suitable solemnity.

I looked at the time: we were due to meet Jérémie in half an hour.

"I hope you're the type of guy who gets a move on … "

He stood up, heroic and impassive, crossed the café under the watching eyes of the waiters, approached the two girls, whispered something in their ears; it was then that his expression froze, he swallowed hard, gave an embarrassed smile, turned on his heel, walked up to me and said, still standing:

"Right, come on, we're going."

I could hardly stop myself from laughing.

"What did they say to you?"

He waited until we were out of the café before replying.

"They told me to piss off! Can you imagine? I've hit an all-time low! Whores tell me to piss off … "

"But what did they say to you?"

"Nothing! They just sent me packing. Sluts … "

He didn't seem to find it amusing.

"Look, they just weren't prostitutes, that's all."

"But they were, I'm certain! Only, I don't know why, they just wouldn't."

He was furious. And I saw something very menacing in his eyes, a kind of hatred, it seemed to me, that was directed not against those two girls in particular, but against the whole of humanity, and at that moment I thought I glimpsed the man he truly was, and it frightened me.

"All this because of Flaubert!" I said in the end, to defuse the atmosphere a little.

3

THE CASINO BAR

JÉRÉMIE WAS WAITING for us in the lobby. We left the hotel and took a taxi. Cairo is a city in which it is practically impossible to walk. What's more, in certain districts the pavements are ridiculously narrow. People drive fast, often very badly, and there are numerous accidents. In Cairo, pedestrians are living under a death sentence. Jérémie got into the front seat of the taxi and gave the driver directions. Then, turning towards us, he explained that just lately, after Chirac's stand against the war in Iraq, the fact of being French really made life easier.

"People feel betrayed by Mubarak because he followed the American line unquestioningly. In fact, they had the clear impression that it was the Americans who were making the decisions for them. And it's understandable that there's something vaguely unpleasant about the idea of being led by cretins … "

"Vaguely, yes … "

"In any event, it was like a divorce between the people and the government. As a reaction, there's also been a sort of surge in international Muslim solidarity. In the last year, for example, it's incredible how many more veiled women there are! Everyone will tell you that. People don't realise, I think, when they see things from a foreign perspective. But when you've been on the spot for a while, you notice it straight away, I can tell you. In any case, as far as most people were concerned, France was the only country that defended their interests. Consequently, I found on several occasions that a taxi driver would waive the fare for a journey just because I'd told him I was French. I even had English friends who passed themselves off as French … "

"Isn't that the case any more?" I asked him.

"Things have changed a bit over the last few weeks. Because of the law on secularism. Here, people thought it was an anti-Islamic law, banning the wearing of the veil in the street … That's why, just for the time being, it's better not to say you're French."

Martin wasn't listening to the discussion. He stayed in the background, looking out of the window. At that moment I realised he had felt humiliated in the hotel garden. His reaction seemed excessive to me. Jérémie showed us a street at the end of which his apartment was located. Then, a little further on, the journalists' trade union. The building couldn't be used for much, since the press was entirely in State hands. Any journalist who didn't write exactly what he was supposed to lost his job immediately, that's what I'd been told. This led to some rather curious things. For example, all the dailies led on Mubarak every day, as if international news was essentially to be deduced from his movements. I had spotted this headline, in *Al-Arham*, the newspaper I had found in my room when I arrived at the hotel: "Meeting with Bush: Mubarak agrees to give his opinion on the international situation." In that context, it's true, it was hard to imagine any purpose for a union of 'journalists'.

"Right, anyway, do you feel a bit more rested now?" Jérémie asked with plastic-coated enthusiasm.

"A bit," replied Martin in a sombre voice.

The taxi dropped us off at a mosque built of alabaster. I was happy to be back in this city: the Khan el-Khalili souk, the noise and dust of Tahrir Square, the central railway station and above all these splendid mosques, gradually crumbling away, day after day.

"I adore this country," I said to Martin then.

The restaurant where we'd arranged to meet was in the souk, a few minutes away. It was a traditional restaurant, with quite a reputation. To get to it, we had to cross several of those alleyways where the traders grab you by the arm and try to sell you some stupid trinket using rather original arguments, such as: "It's cheaper than free!" Jérémie led us to the restaurant without any difficulty. His friends were already waiting for us inside. We said our hellos. Thibault and Paul. Nice to meet you. They both worked at the Embassy and had lived in Cairo for almost three years. They were about our age. We ordered *mezzes*. As regards drinks, we had a choice of a multitude of fruit juices; however, alcohol was not served. For me, a dinner without wine wasn't really a dinner, but fine, once again it was cultural.

"It's no joking matter for them," Thibault explained. "To give you an example, the street the restaurant stands in is named after an Egyptian from goodness knows when who cut his son's throat because he found him drunk … "

"Really? In that case, perhaps we will have fruit juice."

The discussion was quite enjoyable, essentially led by Thibault, who had the soul of a TV presenter: he could talk for hours without anybody really realising. It was an entirely bearable background noise. Regarding the veil, they confirmed what everyone was saying: the phenomenon was gaining ground in a worrying way. And, according to them, it was an international phenomenon.

"Today, all these countries have become a prison for women and maintain a hatred of sex! People tell themselves it goes without saying, but it hasn't always been like that. Think of the *Thousand and One Nights*! When I arrived here, three years ago, I reread the story, I'd forgotten how racy it was … "

Martin's head finally emerged from his dinner.

"Really?"

"There are some unsurpassable erotic scenes. It's magnificent! Anyway, not very long ago, the text was banned by the Egyptian authorities with the sole aim of placating the Islamic fundamentalists! Do you realise that?"

"It's mad!"

"Most of all it's very worrying. But the real question, as I see it, is how we've travelled from a culture that extolled the virtues of sexual ardour to such an obvious negation of sex. That's all."

Wasn't he exaggerating a little? I asked him if he didn't think that sex was as omnipresent as elsewhere, but that it was simply hidden. I could easily imagine lovers furtively embracing, in the shadow of the Koran's rigid morality. He answered that this was often what people said, but that he didn't believe it. Islam had succeeded in its attempt to regulate social life completely. After living here for three years, he could virtually state it as a fact: outside marriage, there was no sex in this country! Nothing! It was a sexual desert!

"But just now in our hotel," objected Martin, "you couldn't help noticing as we were going that there were one or two whores around … "

"Yes, as we were going," I said, aiming the words at Martin, but he pretended he hadn't heard me.

"They're not Egyptian women. They are often Lebanese or Moroccan, but they are not Egyptian. And they only sleep with Saudis, I believe. In any event, for Egyptians there is no prostitution and no sexual freedom."

"What do they do?" lamented Martin.

"They bugger each other."

Apart from that, the food was excellent.

I was rather surprised by what Thibault had said. I couldn't
see how a human community could keep going without sex.
The frustration must be gigantic. I had often heard tell of
an ersatz homosexuality intended to make up for the lack of
women, but I had no idea if it was myth or reality. From what
I'd been told, curious as it might seem, virtually the same
phenomenon was found in certain ultra-Catholic families in
Versailles. On no account did the girls want to lose their virginity before marriage. That's why, during their adolescence,
they got their lovers to sodomise them. In a more general
way, religious extremism always leads to these sorts of hypocritical aberrations.

For a long time in the West, abstinence was regarded as the
most reliable way of saving one's soul. Religion had the particular function of structuring collective life around certain
values, and this could only exclude sexuality from the social
arena. I would imagine that, for centuries, people's inner lives
were virtually limited to a feeble struggle against their own
impulses. At the same time, as Thibault had recalled, the
East had the *Thousand and One Nights*. Which moreover served
as a pretext for the great crusades. Several historians have
indeed demonstrated that the theme of Muslim 'luxury' had
served as a stimulus to religious conquests. (I then thought of
Nietzsche's words in *The Antichrist*: "Later on the crusaders
fought something, whereas they would have done better to
prostrate themselves in the dust before it … ") Then, little by
little, the West rid itself of this frigid religion and developed
a more tragic view of existence: the absence of transcend-
ence ensured that the pleasure of the moment regained all
its former importance. To the despair of the priests, one
must experience pleasure here and now. While one waited
for death.

Today the Islamic world looks very sternly upon the West,
which represents everything that is reprehensible in its eyes:

debauchery, frenzy and decadence. So we find our situations reversed: as in the age of the crusades, the theme of Western luxury serves as an argument for Islamic Jihad. I thought back to the article I had read on the plane about Tariq Ramadan. He clearly thought that Islam was going to bring spiritual renewal to the West. For him, Islam had a vocation to proliferate and, in reaction to this ambition, people were more and more frequently heard saying that if something decisive didn't happen, Western civilisation quite simply had no chance.

The conversation was now revolving around a girl called Lamia, a girl from the Embassy.

"Who is she, this Lamia?" I asked, in a bid to get back into the discussion.

"You'll meet her tomorrow at the book fair. She works with us. She's the prettiest girl in Cairo … "

"Tomorrow?" noted Martin, innocently.

After dinner Thibault, who had tirelessly hosted the evening, suggested that we should go and smoke some *chicha*. I declined the invitation, choosing instead to return to the hotel. Martin decided to come with me. We took a taxi from outside the mosque. The trip cost us about fifteen Egyptian pounds. In the hotel lobby, Martin suggested we should visit the bar at the casino before going up to our rooms. It wasn't a bad idea. And a moment later, we found ourselves in a large, over-lit room.

I'd always had a tendency to gamble. I was particularly fond of poker and roulette. After changing some money into dollars, I settled myself at a table, a vodka on the rocks in my hand. The room was essentially filled with obese, vulgar Saudis. Islam's debauchees. Girls were waiting at the bar. Martin sipped a whisky opposite me. He didn't want to gamble and was content to watch me. He preferred to save his dough for something else, he said, turning towards the bar; he really wasn't giving up.

"Thibault told you they only sleep with the Saudis!"

"No … they're whores."

As usual, I bet on twenty-six; and thus lost two hundred dollars in half an hour. But doubtless I was asking for it. During this time, I saw Martin approach the bar, and it seemed to me, from a distance, that he spoke with one of the girls.

"Now, imagine what you could have done with that money," he told me once he was back at the table.

"That's true. A smoke … "

"Without fire! It's a pointless waste of money."

"You're only saying that because you're not a gambler."

"I am a gambler. Only I'm poor."

"So am I."

"Then you're stupid. You can't be a gambler and poor at the same time. Unless you're stupid."

"So … "

"So what?"

"The girl! What did you say to her?"

Relishing the moment, he signalled to me that we should leave the room. I downed the rest of my second vodka in a single gulp. This guy really was beginning to make me laugh.

"I walked past her," he explained in a whisper, as if it were a real confession, "she smiled at me, I thought I had nothing to lose, so I went towards her and gave her a scrap of paper I'd written my room number on."

"Is that all?"

"No! Because she spoke perfect French. She must be Lebanese. She was a bit shocked. She told me: 'We're not in France here, things don't happen like that here.' I told her I was sorry, that I'd seen her smile and couldn't resist the urge to come over and talk to her."

41

"And then?"

"She explained that here things proceed at a gentle pace. You have to sit down, have a chat, buy the girl a drink, you see what I'm on about? Pretend you're thinking about something else, always the same hypocrisy … Can you imagine, even with the whores here, you have to pretend!"

"It's cultural!" I said, with irony.

"So I made my excuses. And that's when she asked me to give her my room number again."

"So she's going to join you later?"

"That's what I'm thinking."

He seemed happy, and I couldn't prevent myself laughing. And yet he was rather pathetic. In the lift, I told him that I hoped at least that he hadn't made a mistake with the room number and given her mine for example.

"And you'd complain about that, would you?"

"Ah, but you do realise you're about to fuck with the Embassy's daily expenses … ?"

"Well, yes! At the expense of the French taxpayer! To whom, let us note as we go, we are also indebted for financing your complete failure at the roulette table!"

"That's true … "

So we improvised a minute's silence in homage to the French taxpayer.

"You know, I've never understood people who kick up a fuss because they reckon there are too many taxes," Martin went on " … Me, I reckon taxes are really useful. And here's the proof!"

He was manifestly in a very good mood.

I stayed for a while on the balcony of my room. There was no strong alcohol in the mini bar. Certain Muslims are very generous: the laws they impose upon themselves, they want to impose on you too. In truth, in a dramatically individualistic era, few people display such ardour for your salvation; it's rather nice. I asked at reception if someone could bring me a vodka. It arrived within ten minutes. I thought back over the day, the host of impressions that are contained within the first few hours of a journey. Then I thought about my parents. Travelling down the Nile with them. Our stay at a fine hotel in Luxor. My brother had filmed it all. Some of the footage must still exist. I don't think I shall ever be able to watch that film.

I closed the sliding glass door, and sat down at the desk. I wanted to write something. I told myself that Martin must still be waiting for his Lebanese girl. No doubt he'd taken a shower, and now he was waiting. Perhaps in the same position as me. With the same feeling of lassitude. The same melancholy. The thought came to me that I should go down and look for a girl. Suddenly someone knocked at my door, and my heart skipped a beat. I swallowed hard and went to open the door.

There was nobody there. I looked to the left and right. Nobody. I went back to my desk, feeling a little anxious. I picked up the hotel's headed notepaper. My mind wandered for a long time. Then I wrote a letter to Jeanne, and went to bed.

4

NOISES OF WAR

THE TELEPHONE RANG. It was time to get up. We were due to meet the guide for our visit to the Cairo Museum. Still tormented by insomnia, I had practically not closed my eyes all night. All in all I had perhaps slept for two hours—which had left me the time to leaf through a little of the Koran and to annotate a few particularly unpoetic passages. It wasn't a discovery in the true sense of the word: I had already read it in the days when I was very interested in the comparative history of religions. I told myself that those who claim that the Koran invites one only to love and that only a 'certain interpretation' of the text leads sometimes to contempt for women and violence, that those people simply have never read the Koran or are afraid of saying the wrong thing. In any event, I told myself again, it is now impossible to say anything about it. Silence alone reigns. I even reread the following out loud: *Admonish those women whom you fear are unfaithful; relegate them to separate rooms and beat them*—Koran, *sura* 4, verse 34.

I got up. I switched on the TV to see if there was a twenty-four-hour news channel. Then I went to have a shower. I didn't think of Martin again until a little later. What had happened to him? I dialled his room number. Nobody picked up the phone. Doubtless he was waiting for me downstairs.

I had turned off the sound on the TV, but just as I was about to switch off the set, the pictures drew my attention.

A catastrophe had occurred, but I couldn't identify what it was. People were running about in all directions. Bodies were being brought out of dusty rubble. There was smoke. Women were weeping in front of the cameras. I stood there fascinated, open-mouthed, for at least ten minutes. Shit, I told myself. It must be a terrorist attack. A shiver of horror ran through me.

I went down to the restaurant. Martin was already seated at a table, reading the newspaper. I asked a waitress to bring me some coffee, and sat down opposite him.

"So? Did you have a good night?"

"Not bad, and you?"

He didn't look in a very good mood.

"I saw on the TV that something has happened … Some kind of terrorist attack, I think. Did they say anything about it?"

"Yes, they did … But it's not a terrorist attack. An apartment block collapsed."

"All on its own? I mean … "

"Yes, yes … All on its own. It was too old."

"Where was that?"

"In the centre of Cairo. Forty dead, apparently."

The Egyptians really weren't having any luck at the moment. I got up to go and choose my breakfast. The buffet was copious, but I didn't fancy any of it. Everything was greasy. Beside me, a woman was having a second helping of sugary cakes. I turned round and went back to sit down. I noticed that Cotté was seated at a table with another guy not too far from us. Both were wearing Vichy blue short-sleeved shirts. I felt tired just thinking about spending the morning with them. In any event, I don't know why, I had a bad feeling about this day.

"Well, aren't you going to tell me?" I asked Martin finally.

"Tell you what?"

The waitress brought my coffee.

"Honestly! About the girl ... Did she come?"

"No. I waited a while, and then I went to bed."

"Yeah?"

"But I could have predicted it: I was just a lifeline for her. A backup solution. In case no Saudi took her. You see, I don't know how much they give them, those stupid fat bastards, but in my opinion it represents a fair amount of cash. So obviously she wasn't going to come and earn a pittance with me ... "

"So what did you do?" I asked him, to try and make him a little less ill at ease.

"I had a wank," he replied calmly. "It's the best thing to do, when you discover you have a hard-on."

I pretended to laugh. Then he explained to me that he had nonetheless been interested to see how things were going in the casino bar. According to him, there was one positive sign there: after all, all those Saudis heralded the inevitable failure of Islam. I couldn't quite see how. "You know what Mohammed promises to the faithful? An exotic, sensual paradise where young girls surrender themselves easily! A sort of gigantic easy lay. Well, all of that already exists in this world! The frenzy of consumption and sex that characterises the West today is in direct competition with Mohammed's paradise: you have to choose between the two, and all those Saudis have clearly made their choice. If they're acting like this, they're no longer hoping to go to paradise; they'd rather get drunk immediately on forbidden pleasures. Really, one might even doubt their true faith. They are extremists in their country because that suits them, but the thing they really aspire to is basically what Western capitalism offers. In the end, all these guys will abandon Islam ... "

I didn't agree with him. Debauchery and hypocrisy did not in any way herald the death knell of the Muslim system.

True, the West exercised an attraction for privileged young Arabs, but all the same they weren't renouncing Muslim values. Moreover, taking a slightly extreme example, the terrorists who had sadly become famous after September 11th had all more or less integrated into the Western system before desiring its destruction. "That's not untrue," he said after a moment's reflection. A few years ago, one might have believed that all religions were in the end condemned to death as a system for explaining the world, principally because of capitalism, which directly combats religious puritanism by exacerbating desire, the will to consume and materialism. But eventually the opposite assessment became obvious! "It's true," he went on, "the world is becoming more radical ... The United States are crudely governed by the Evangelical sect while, on the other hand, Islam is hardening and preparing an army of uncultivated types who dream of only one thing: destroying us ... "

I then talked to him about the passages of the Koran that I had read during the night. He seemed astonished. He hadn't seen the package in his room. From memory, I recited the *suras* calling for the extermination of infidels ... He listened to me without saying a word. I believe he was thinking about something else. Then we went down to the lobby. The guide was already there. A short while after, Monsieur Cotté arrived. After the introductions had been made, the guide suggested that we leave the hotel: the Embassy's car was waiting for us. Classy, or what.

It was only nine o'clock in the morning, but it was already very hot. It was just at that moment that I realised we were in Africa; I've always been rather slow on the uptake about these kinds of thing. The traffic was impossible. The guide explained to us that it was because of the apartment building that had collapsed. Martin didn't speak. Doubtless he'd had insufficient sleep. As for Monsieur Cotté, he was holding forth on the Pyramids. He had visited them the previous day. It had been a real aesthetic shock for him: they were a lot smaller than in his imagination!

"So, you're writing a book on Alexandria then?"

"How did you know that?"

"The Embassy official told me."

"He did? Yes, about Alexandria … I've always adored libraries."

" … "

"Haven't you ever seen it? You should, it's impressive! To tell you the truth, it's a lot bigger than I was expecting!"

Monsieur Cotté was a man of nuances; this was doubtless how he came to have important responsibilities in politics. He set off on a long monologue on the symbolic impact of this immense library, bringing together the works of all countries and in all languages. To listen to him, you'd think it was a source of hope for humanity. In any event, he already had his promotional arguments ready.

The driver set us down in Tahrir Square, opposite the Museum. Curiously, I had a quite precise memory of the place, which was the very embodiment of mystery and beauty. The exhibition rooms on the ground floor were organised in a chronological manner. Cotté, standing admiringly before a monumental statue of Khephren depicting a woman with an Egyptian crown, said: "You see, it's interesting, even back then they were wearing the veil!"

"In fact," the guide cut in with slight embarrassment, "what you can see is a classic crown of the Fourth Dynasty, but it is not a religious sign. It is Muslims who wear the veil … "

"Yes, yes, that's true. But back then, weren't there any Muslims in Egypt yet?"

Nobody informed him that he was making a slight error

of more than two thousand years; but that can happen to anyone, apparently. The first floor was essentially devoted to the tomb of Tutankhamun. I learned that this prince had died at the age of nineteen—he was a bit like an Egyptian Radiguet, with the exception that he hadn't written anything. Moreover, he hadn't done anything special. It was just that his tomb was still intact when it was discovered in the nineteen-twenties. It contained an incredible number of objects, among them—and this is what most captured my attention—a minuscule condom made of silk! The thing seemed unfeasible to me.

"It's mad, isn't it?"

"It's true that it's astonishing … "

"I didn't think they already had condoms back then!"

"Forgive the cliché, but it's a little bizarre when you see that the women are almost all veiled today! Whereas three thousand years ago, the distinction between the principle of pleasure and that of reproduction was apparently obvious!"

"Yeah. All the same, it's one heck of a regressive step … "

"Islam … "

"A 'certain interpretation' of Islam!" the man of nuances corrected him.

After lunch we went to the book event, which was outside the city in Heliopolis. The trip lasted the best part of an hour because of the traffic jams. The air conditioning had stopped working, and the driver opened the window: after ten minutes, we were all coughing our lungs up because of the pollution. Jérémie then informed me that the French civil servants who worked in this city were paid a pollution bonus for their retirement.

"Have you prepared anything for the lecture?" Martin asked me without Jérémie hearing.

"Not really. But it's not necessary. There'll be a female moderator ... "

"A what?"

"A girl who asks us questions. You won't be asked to do a twenty-minute monologue on your vision of literature for example."

"So much the better; that suits me ... "

As I understood it, there was to be a debate with Egyptian novelists and critics. It was bound to be interesting. To be frank, I knew nothing about this country's literature. The only Egyptian writer I had ever read had been living in France for years. I'm talking about Albert Cossery. I often bumped into him around the rue Jacob. He walked with lit-tle, sparrow-like steps, never looking around him. Sometimes you had the impression that the world no longer interested him. I think he was living in a local hotel, the Louisiane, thus renewing the link with that bygone age, the Thirties, when foreign writers lived in Paris hotels, Faulkner at the Lenox, Hemingway at the Ritz—all those fabulous places that are now besieged by American tourists.

"So who is the moderator?" asked Martin. "Is it the famous Lamia?"

"No, she's the editor-in-chief of a vaguely intellectual newspaper. I don't know her," Jérémie added.

Martin looked disappointed; he would have liked to be moderated by Lamia. To our right, Jérémie then showed us what was known as the 'city of the dead'. It was a poor district of Cairo, a former cemetery in which people who couldn't afford a decent place to live had set up home. Entire families lived like this in caves, among the dead.

Throughout the entire journey, I thought of Jeanne. What was she doing? I had deliberately decided not to bring my mobile with me. Now she seemed so far away. Today, I must post the letter I'd written her. After rereading it perhaps, for the vodka had no doubt made me say some clumsy things. She and I wrote to each other a lot. In the early days I was afraid; I'd just emerged from a series of violent disappointments. I was at a low ebb. Then I met her, this really marvellous girl, and yes—something in me was afraid of the promises of suffering this represented. Mustn't get too attached, I told myself stupidly. Barricade myself in against the pain. "You'll leave me," I told her sometimes. This amused her.

"Why do you say that?"

"Because. I know. One day, you will leave me."

"So you know the future, do you?"

"Yes. Don't you believe me?"

She didn't believe me. And then, I remember it perfectly, I picked up an empty envelope.

"See this envelope? Inside it, I'm going to write the exact conditions of our break-up. I'm even going to give you a date. Tell you how things are going to happen, what you'll say to me, what I'll say to you, everything! The future, basically. I'm going to seal this envelope, and you're not to read it until the moment comes, right? And you'll see."

She laughed.

"But you do promise me you won't open it before, don't you?"

She promised. And yet, several days after this discussion, I found the scrap of paper on which I'd written our downfall; it was lying around, forgotten, on the corner of a table. This made me angry. I told her off for not playing the game right to the end, but she wouldn't admit anything:

"I'm telling you, I didn't read your letter!"

To prove it to me, she showed me the envelope: she had carefully stored it among her things the way a little girl would do; and indeed, it had not been opened. I realised then that I had forgotten to put the letter into the envelope. That was the only explanation. At first this seemed impossible, but I had to face up to it: the envelope with our future in it was empty.

"Do you think it's a sign?" she asked me, laughing.

It seems to me that it was then that we got into the habit of writing to each other a lot. To fill up this emptiness, perhaps. And to forget what I had written, imbecile that I was, on that scrap of paper we'd swiftly burnt. She signed her letters: 'your ladybird'.

It's the telephone, and in particular the mobile, that has killed off the art of letter-writing once and for all. I often think of those women who lived in hope, with the pledge of one single love letter, when the other person, for example, went off to war. Back then, words had a formidable strength, since they decided lives. People waited, and trusted, even without news of the other person, for infinite lengths of time. Today, you start panicking the moment you can't get that other person on your mobile. What's he doing? Why isn't she answering? Who's he with? Anxiety has gained ground. We have entered a period of no return that signals the end of waiting, that is, of trust and of silence.

The book event was in reality a sort of immense fair. The majority of the books being exhibited were religious: commentaries on the verses, methods of renunciation, prayer guides. Away to one side, the place allocated to literature was minuscule. "Here, people don't read novels at all," Jérémie explained to me. "With regard to literature, at the extreme end there's a small elite interested in poetry, but that's all … "

At last I realised why Martin and I had been invited.

The room in which we were supposed to give our talk was, however, quite full. The other participants were waiting for us. We were given simultaneous translation headphones so that we could follow the conversation in Arabic. I was seated next to a young male novelist, aged around thirty, who didn't greet me. The moderator began immediately and, contrary to what I had thought, she arbitrarily called upon Martin to give us his vision of literature in a few, well-chosen words. The poor guy swallowed hard and started to mumble, all the more so because each sentence was instantly translated into Arabic. Then the discussion got underway. The moderator spoke French rather badly, but thought she spoke it very well; as a result, she regularly asked us questions along these lines:

"In France, are young writers younger than those who write and are older than the young ones?"

Or: "Do you think that the authors who have influenced you influenced your writing?"

The audience viewed us seriously; these were important questions, after all. Working hard to answer ("The new generation? I've always approached it from behind, but not every day ... "), I scanned the room to see which one might be Lamia. From what Jérémie had told me, she was Moroccan and had been working with them for only six months. I'd got the impression that he liked her a lot, and that he wasn't the only one. Thibault too was vaguely in her thrall. Martin soon would be too. "The most beautiful woman in Cairo." It has to be said that the competition wasn't very fierce and that she had a sort of monopoly in the capital, since apparently Egyptian women, even when they were not veiled, did not sleep with anyone.

After a while, most of the opportunities to talk were granted to the two critics who were among those taking part—two types of prehistoric tortoise, working on the two big national dailies. Listening to them talk, I realised that they were in reality civil servants, since the press belonged to the State, and that in this respect they were its representatives. "The most important consideration when judging a text," said one of them, "is morality and beauty. Is a novel moral? And can it make that morality aesthetic? Those are the questions that the criticism asks!" (In my earpiece, the woman translating his words into French said 'criticism' instead of 'critic', no doubt because of the English 'criticism'; in any event, we weren't that far from 'cretinism'. Then Martin intervened, through a taste for provocation, and asked the two cretins what they thought of Flaubert. In his mind, he was probably alluding to the *Correspondence*, assuming that they would at least have heard of the Egyptian passages which, as we've seen, don't entirely embody morality, but they replied with direct reference to *Madame Bovary*, doubtless the only one of the author's books that they'd read. I thus learned that this novel had been translated into Arabic, but that this was not a reason for reading it. Such a text was contrary to ethics and aesthetics, the other critic told us. All this pointless bed-hopping! Serious newspapers could certainly not be relied upon to defend it! Death to *Madame Bovary*! I was nevertheless rather stunned. (It's a good job these guys haven't read my books, I told myself.) At the time when it was published, this novel had posed a few problems for Flaubert, whose work had allegedly outraged public and religious morality, but that was in 1856! People still have the impression that Egypt is a very pretty country with its pyramids and its sunsets over the Nile, but we forget a little too swiftly that it is also a country in which *Madame Bovary*, the story of that woman with her unhappy marriage, her mediocre husband and her pointless lovers, questions the order of things too closely to be read. Here, marriages are necessarily good, husbands are never mediocre and lovers don't exist.

I thought back to what Thibault had told us: the tales of the *Thousand and One Nights* had also been banned. After the discussion, I met a female journalist who spoke very good

French and seemed to come from another planet, the planet of civilisation. I told her how surprised I was about what had been said regarding Flaubert. She had studied in France and understood what I was talking about. "Unfortunately that's how it is," she lamented, "you can't do anything about it, and it's getting worse and worse." The young Egyptian novelist was standing next to us. He spoke a little English. I asked him how a person could write, if it meant submitting in such a docile manner to religious morality. He looked sad. He explained to me that, in his opinion, there was really no literature in this country. "Islam is incompatible with real literature," he said, doubtless exaggerating a little. The official writers produced detached lyricism based on heritage and the Pyramids, and the hierarchy applauded them and gave them medals; as for the real writers, they left for other countries, if they had the opportunity, or—as he did—wrote poetry, which was not subject to such censure because it was less clear and therefore less dangerous. I thought again of Tutankhamun's condom.

"The really scary thing," Martin added, "is seeing that it's getting more and more like that in Europe."

"More like what?"

"They're bringing their bloody religious morality back to us!"

I was a little embarrassed. Why was Martin so aggressive?

"They call it the West's 'spiritual renewal'! When it's just the opposite of spiritual! Did you hear what they said? The impossibility of writing about anything except what's beautiful and good, well frankly, that's tantamount to the death of the spirit. And it's already started! The mind and spirit pose a direct threat to those who hammer home a single truth that's come straight out of the desert! It's barbarity!"

"Barbarity?"

"Exactly. Barbarity is the end of culture! And the breeding

ground for this barbarity is illiteracy, mental regression and bullshit in all its forms! The number of court cases against books brought by Muslim associations that are haunted by virtue is downright grim! And it's going to get worse and worse!"

I chose not to say anything in reply. But it made me think of Valéry's *Variétés*: and in particular the first letter of *The Spiritual Crisis*, in which the author discovers, in the days following the war, that a civilisation has the same fragility as a life. It is mortal and so it can be stabbed to death by the very person who's walking towards it with a big, moderate smile.

The western Hamlet stands before this forthcoming spectacle. What will he decide to do? He ponders what is coming. As for the ghost, he has the intuition that something serious is being cooked up in the silence of morning. The beating of a skinless drum. He thinks of the fear of one day seeing the death of what he cares about, and on the other hand he also thinks about the madness of wanting unreservedly to embrace the global trend. He totters between the two abysses.

If he chooses a skull, it's a famous skull—*Whose was it?*—this one here was Rabelais. He invented European humour and sent the sheep plunging headlong into the sea without fear of their imbecilic bleating ... And this other skull is that of Voltaire, slightly deformed around the jaw through too much sniggering at religion. That one there actually belonged to Flaubert, who one day wrote:

There are few women whom, in my head at least, I haven't undressed from head to toe!

Hamlet isn't altogether sure what to do with all these skulls. Sometimes he would like to throw them in the faces of certain bearded individuals. But if he abandons them, will he cease to be himself? His appallingly clear-sighted mind contemplates the progression from peace, which he had hoped for with all his heart, to the certainty of war. That's how it is. He can't do anything about it. What's he to do? Yet again he asks himself. Should I follow the movement and imitate Polonius, who is now campaigning for respect for the Other One? Like Laertes, who constantly repeats that one must at all costs rejoice in the future? Like Rosencrantz, who sniggers in my face when I confide my pessimism to him?

"The world doesn't need these ghosts any more," I then said out loud.

Everyone looked at me in astonishment. It's true that I had jumped a stage in my reasoning. Several people were already heading for the exit to go and have a drink in Heliopolis.

"Right then, are we going?" asked Jérémie impatiently.

5

NAKED WOMEN

I DECIDED TO DROP IN at the hotel before going to dinner. I spent a long time alone in my room. If I can't isolate myself for a few hours each day, I become impatient and difficult to live with. I can't live in a community. And besides, I was tired. Basically, I hadn't slept enough since I'd woken up in Paris. I stayed stretched out on my bed, reading, thinking back over it all. Then I took a bath. And I think I dozed a little. Lamia hadn't come to the talk. I would see her that evening. A dinner had been arranged on a boat on the Nile. Jérémie had told me that we'd find alcohol on board. I was supposed to join them there. I got dressed. I can't pack suitcases properly. For example, I regularly forget to take shirts, which often complicates my journeys. But this time I had everything I needed. I hesitated for a moment about going to this dinner. My eyes hurt so much that I wanted to sleep. I called reception, and asked for a vodka to wake me up. At that moment, I saw that the light on my telephone was blinking, and I told myself that I perhaps had a message. I'd better listen to it. It must be Jérémie, telling me that the timetable or the location had changed. No. It was Jeanne. I was happy to hear her voice. But I didn't remember giving her the name of my hotel. She must have called my publisher. So something serious had happened. My heart missed a beat, and I was resigned to hearing the bad news, which was in reality good news: she might have found an apartment. As we didn't have a lot of money, and neither she nor I had a stable job, it was quite difficult to find a trusting landlord. My cheerful ladybird sent me a kiss over the telephone. Somebody knocked. I went to open the door, a smile on my lips: it was room service, bringing me the vodka. It went down well, that one. I went out onto the balcony. I looked at the city, my glass in my hand. It really was good news. One of those bits of news that make you forget, just for a moment, the calm certainty of the unimportance of everything—and I drank to my own health.

On leaving the hotel, I took a taxi and told the driver the name of the restaurant. I just couldn't manage to pronounce that name, and he couldn't understand me, and I had to ask the hotel porter to help me to explain to the driver where I had to go, but the porter—who didn't speak English—didn't understand either what I was asking him to do, and had to ask at the reception desk for someone to explain to him where I had to go so that he could in turn explain it to the taxi driver who was to take me there—a moment later, inevitably, I was in front of the Ramses.

This was a sort of boat moored alongside the quay, transformed into a restaurant: from the bank, an illuminated walkway gave access to the boat. It was quite pretty, and I wasn't at all tired any more. A veiled woman opened the door for me. She was rather cute—at least, as far as you could tell. She led me to the table reserved by the Embassy. Jérémie was already there with Martin.

"Did you find it easily?" he asked me.

"No problem. And what about you, did you get that *chicha*?"

"We went into a bar in Heliopolis."

A waiter brought us a tray with glasses of all colours.

"It's the aperitif," explained Jérémie. "Fruit juices ... Here, they serve alcohol during the meal."

"Hello ... "

A young woman was standing in front of me. Jérémie proceeded to do the introductions: she was called Mathilde. She also worked at the Embassy and, incidentally, had a face like a sea monster. We shook hands. She had been at the talk and had very much liked what I said about the new realism. This was even nicer of her seeing as I hadn't said anything about the new realism. Next, the cultural attaché, Jérémie's superior, came up. He greeted me with great refinement; I realised that I was supposed to be honoured to meet him. Then we drank to Egypt, where, without a doubt, French-speaking culture was very poorly represented. The cultural attaché launched into a discussion on Stendhal, a short passage of whose work he claimed to read every morning. We were still waiting for a few guests. The table laid for us was indeed quite large. The cultural attaché's wife was rushing about all over the place and explained that it was she who had had the idea of holding the dinner in this restaurant, and not at their home; this seemed to make her happy. The two Egyptian novelists were talking to another girl, but I could only see her back and her long dark hair—this was probably the famous Lamia.

Jérémie was talking to me about the following day's programme, but I was only listening with one ear. I sipped my fruit juice in silence. As I understood it, in the morning we had a chance to visit the Pyramids. I had already seen them, and I think I said I'd rather not go back. In a general way, I can't rid myself of the slightly puerile disgust that tourism arouses in me. My glass was empty, and a waiter came to take it from my hand. At the same moment, Lamia approached us. Without even looking at me, she asked Jérémie if he knew who the last guests were. Then she noticed that I existed, gave me a cold smile and asked me, with a slight Arabic accent, how my first day in Cairo had gone.

"My second day," I corrected her.

She had large dark eyes that were not afraid to look another person full in the face. Her hair fell prettily onto her shoulders, and she was charming, but less beautiful than I'd been expecting. After all, they'd said: "The most beautiful woman in Cairo."

"Have you been to Egypt before, Monsieur—?"

I was surprised by the formality of her tone. We were about the same age.

"Yes. Once. But that was a tourist visit, and it was quite a long time ago … "

She gave me a polite smile, but didn't give a damn what I said, and that was fine by me.

"What really surprised me," I went on, mainly for the benefit of Jérémie, "was what I heard earlier, at the discussion … "

"What?"

"About Flaubert! I hadn't imagined things had got so … Because through Flaubert, in the end it's the whole of the West they're condemning!"

"You look as if you've only just realised … Those are noises of war!" commented Jérémie.

I wanted to explain to Lamia what had been said, but she interrupted me immediately: she had been there.

"At least censorship in literature isn't the worst kind!" she said. "It's in the media that it's becoming catastrophic!"

"Oh, really?"

"To give you just one example: I believe you're doing a radio interview tomorrow."

Jérémie, who had suddenly become timid, shook his head: in the end the show had been cancelled.

"It's one of the flagship shows on national radio. Well, the radio station has its premises in the same building as the Ministry of the Interior … "

"That is indeed bizarre … "

"And the guy who was going to interview you actually has

two jobs … He's a radio star, yes. But he's also … a general in the police!"

"No?"

"Yes."

She finally managed the ghost of a slightly more sincere smile. But already her eyes were searching the back of the room: the last guests were arriving. She promptly rushed towards them to welcome them. From a distance, I recognised Monsieur Cotté.

We took our seats. I contrived to be next to Jérémie, as I wanted to talk to him. Unfortunately for me, the cultural attaché's wife stationed herself on my right. Cotté positioned himself at the other end of the table, and I saw Lamia once again hurrying to sit next to him. Her stratagem seemed a little vulgar to me. It's true that Cotté was a man worth having in your pocket, if you were a girl with ambitions to get into politics. It was obvious that she knew exactly what she wanted; I would even say that she was the perfect embodiment of the slightly haughty, ambitious woman. And I wondered what they all made of her.

During dinner, Jérémie told me a little about his life in Paris. I wanted to know why he'd decided to go off and spend two years abroad, since he claimed to have no ambitions to be an international diplomat. He then told me that he had left on a sudden whim. To cure himself of a love affair, he admitted almost immediately. "The girl was really quite unbelievable. When I met her, she was already living with a guy. An idiot—as if by chance. For six months, she was continually leaving him, arguing with me, going back to him, leaving me again … I was exhausted. It's a bit pathetic, but I don't think I've ever suffered so much. I didn't even know anybody could suffer that much, I mean, that it was *physically* possible."

He seemed quite upset, and I poured him a little more wine. In fact, I was astonished at the ease with which he was entrusting us with these confidences. Me, I'd have made up another story, an easy pretext, something—me, I'd have lied. In any event, I wouldn't have confided my suffering to anyone, so that I could be absolutely certain of not seeking either to exploit it or degrade it. I've always been surprised by this collective insistence on airing one's problems, upsets and worries. Everyone thinks he has to come out with it in broad daylight. Today, everybody dreams of having a public soul.

So I might have been irritated by what Jérémie was saying. However, as I listened to him, I realised that I was coming to like him more and more. Not everyone would head for the other side of the world to escape from a woman, after all. One must have a certain capacity for suffering. I'd have liked to tell him it was best to keep this suffering quiet, keep it to oneself so as not to spoil it. That it should confine itself to sharpening the attention we pay to things, to the smallest object, to the least coincidence, that it should restore to each of our torn-up moments the profundity and plenitude which our way of life has taken away from them—but secretly.

"She was one of those girls who are a bit crazy," he continued, "a girl who was always going out to nightclubs, who was completely out of it, she was burning up her life, and everything else around it. The opposite of the type that interests me, as a rule. Basically, I think the capacity to love someone almost never holds out against that eccentric kind of life. And she was one of those profoundly egocentric modern women who've become incapable of love, because they're too obsessed with themselves! For my part, I loved her as much as I loathed her. So the best thing, you see, was to get myself away from her. And as far away as possible."

"In any case," Martin said solemnly, "things are the other way round today. It's the men who've become romantic … "

I found this interjection quite surprising. Especially coming from him. (Then I remembered that in one of his novels, the first I think, the central character swiftly assumes the nickname—a subtle literary allusion—of 'Jean-Foutre la Bite' ... John Fuck the Cock ... a great romantic.)

"And then? The very fact of leaving ... "

"Yes, it liberated me, that's for sure. Even if I shall always be choking back sobs for that girl ... "

I wanted to grab another bottle of wine. But the cultural attaché's wife, who'd been trying to enter the discussion for the best part of twenty minutes, grabbed it before I did and filled all our glasses. This was a dream occasion for her. So we had to exchange a few sentences, drink to her hospitality and her exceptional idea of holding the dinner in this restaurant, and not at her home. (On the other side of the table, I heard Cotté talking about Juppé, who was one of his friends. He considered the case against Juppé completely over the top! According to him, the judiciary was waging war on the polity! This was his pet theory; Lamia found it discerning, personal and doubtless very well-founded ...) The attaché's wife then started a discussion in Arabic with one of the Egyptian writers, and our conversation could at last recommence:

"Afterwards I met another girl," continued Jérémie. "A French girl who works at the Centre Français in Alexandria. We were together two months. It was really good. Except at the end when it was a catastrophe. We'd gone to Aswan for a few days. A holiday by the lake. She sulked practically the whole trip. A horrible business. In fact it was already buggered. But I didn't want to admit it to myself ... And when we got back, she told me it was over."

"And you still see her?"

"Not that much. But it's fine! I'm not sad. It's mainly her body I miss ... "

"In any event," commented Martin, who had drunk too much, "I get the impression that in Egypt, it's bodies that everyone misses! You, for example, you've never slept with an Egyptian girl … "

"No. I told you, that doesn't happen much."

"Not even with a … "

Jérémie was a little embarrassed.

"Huh?"

"In your opinion, can a westerner screw a whore?"

An idiotic laugh originated at the back of Jérémie's nose in response to the word 'whore'. He wasn't accustomed to talking about these things so plainly. He darted a worried look at the attaché's wife to make sure she hadn't heard anything.

"I don't know."

"You don't know?"

"No. But I know a guy who knows a lot about all that stuff, if it interests you … "

"You do?"

"Yes. His name is Essam. A guy who knows everything that happens in Cairo. Now, he can give you an answer … "

"You know what would be good?" Martin went on. "If we were to set up a little tour round the bars and suchlike tonight."

"Tonight? After dinner, you mean?"

"Yes. Why not?"

"I can always call that guy, if you want. But well … "

"Have you got his number with you?"

"Yes. He'll tell you about places where there are dancing girls, all that stuff … "

Martin looked delighted. He started telling us about Aragon and Drieu's trawls around the hostelries of Paris in the Thirties. He was keen to find justification in great literature for his personal obsession—which went to show that he wasn't as comfortable as all that with himself.

After dessert, Jérémie failed to get through to Essam. His voicemail was permanently switched on.

"What we can do is go to a bar I know, and we'll eventually meet up with him ... "

One after another, we got up from the table. Martin was manifestly excited by the idea of this trawl through the seedy underbelly of Cairo. I had also drunk a bit too much. So the worst was to be feared. From the other end of the table, Lamia was looking me straight in the eye. I couldn't understand what she was trying to tell me. As for Cotté, he was in full flow about his theory on the library at Alexandria; it sounded most exciting.

"We'll try to take just the one car," said Jérémie.

"Who's coming with us?"

"I don't know."

Mathilde said she was knackered—which gave me an opportunity to remember that she existed.

"Lamia won't come, I don't think. She never goes out."

"So there'll be just the three of us?"

"Four with Thibault, if he joins us."

All the same, I went to see Lamia to tell her we were leaving. Aren't you coming with us? Cotté seemed to be hanging on her reply. A little awkwardly, she replied that she'd rather go home, as she was tired—but tomorrow perhaps? Then Cotté cut in: "I forgot to ask you: there's a dinner at the ambassador's house tomorrow night ... I won't be accompanied, and I wondered if you might agree to go with me ... "

Lamia gave him a broad smile: "With great pleasure." There was no denying it, she was strong, she obtained everything she wanted. I wondered if she realised that she was in the process of selling herself. Doubtless she didn't. Prostitution is everywhere. What's more, we are all forced, in one way or another, to prostitute ourselves, that is to say, to live according to rules that recall those of prostitution.

On this point, Lamia was no exception: she was even sadly commonplace. They stood up at the same moment, and we headed for the exit. The others were already waiting outside on the footbridge. The crescent moon of Islam was shining in the sky.

"Do you speak Arabic?" I asked Lamia.

"Yes, it's my native language. In fact, my parents are Moroccan. I was born in France, but I have always spoken Arabic with my family."

Directing her words especially at Cotté, she explained that before coming to Cairo, just a few months earlier, she had actually been teaching Arabic in Paris ("At the School of Oriental Languages," she specified with a certain pride) but that what really interested her was politics.

"Yes, we've noticed."

She looked daggers at me. Cotté remained silent, doubtless ill at ease. Then I rejoined Jérémie and the others who were waiting at the side of the road. A taxi stopped a moment later. The three of us piled in. Lamia was now talking with the cultural attaché. She looked at me from a long way off with a certain insistence. She would have her revenge. Yes, she would no doubt exact her revenge, and for her that was the equivalent of desiring me. For she was one of those people, I think, who have to dislike you before they can like you. But I was not unaware that the irritation she aroused in me was first and foremost a way of not admitting to myself that I found her seductive. And inaccessible. So I closed the door of the taxi. Jérémie told the driver the address of the place of perdition, and a moment later we were crossing Cairo at top speed, with the windows open.

6

IN THE MIDDLE OF THE OCEAN

I N THE TAXI, I THOUGHT back to what Martin had told us. I was rather astonished that he should evoke the trawls of Aragon and Drieu, and not those of Flaubert and Du Camp, which as far as we were concerned had the advantage of taking part in the bordellos of Egypt and which, in this respect, could have served us as a poetic reference for the evening, or even—if one admits that things haven't changed that much—a set of instructions. Back then, Flaubert isn't Flaubert yet, but he dreams of becoming a writer, and literature is already being written before their very eyes: on the 6th March 1850, in Esneh, they meet a prostitute from Damascus, Kuchuk Hanem, who has such an impact on them that both will describe her in their respective works (*Le Nil* for Du Camp and *Voyage en Egypte* for Flaubert)—in the same way that orientalist painting and travel writers flattered the eastern feminine universe. But Du Camp is concerned with building himself a good reputation and only publishes toned-down versions of their evening of the 6th March. *Lifting my head, I saw her; it was like an apparition. Standing in the last rays of the sun, which enveloped her in light, dressed in a simple little gauze chemise in a shade of Madeira brown and wide trousers made of white cotton with pink stripes, her feet bare in her* babouches, *her shoulders covered by the swathes of blue silk that formed the tassel of her* tarboosh, *her neck tightly clasped by three necklaces of large beads, her arms encircled by gleaming bracelets, her ears adorned with trapezoidal earrings laden with thin strands of gold, her hair chestnut in colour, plaited and held on the forehead by a black ribbon, white, sturdy, joyful, full of youthfulness and life, she was superb.* As you can see, it's a little short on action.

It is in his *Notes de voyage*, published after his death, that Flaubert describes the same evening with complete freedom. The manuscript was severely censored by his niece. He recounts how he follows this woman into the bowels of a sordid palace. Then, after a lascivious dance, how he consents to several doses of oral sex. I felt ferocious, he says. He speaks also of the tenderness he feels for this prostitute whom he is now watching as she sleeps, holding her hand. He is next to her and thinks of other nights when he watched other women sleeping—and all the other nights he has spent, devoid of sleep. He thinks back over everything, sinks into sadness and reveries—he entertains himself by killing bugs that crawl across the wall, leaving long, blackish-red arabesques on that whitewashed surface. We loved each other, at least I believe we did … I remembered that ambiguous form of words, sublime, elevating that simple screw to another dimension, to the sadness of soon having to part and abandon extreme sensuality, and it was precisely that form of words, added to the precise description of the tumble, that the sinister niece had decided to censor. It was like banning *Madame Bovary*.

I thought back to what Martin had said about the intransigence of Islam with regard to romantic fiction. I wasn't in agreement with him: for me, it wasn't 'stupid religious morality' that was in question, but stupidity full stop, that is to say the certainty of possessing the truth and of denying, in its name, everything that contradicts it. In this respect, Flaubert's niece was as dangerous as the Sheikh of Cairo.

"So what exactly is this place?" bellowed Martin.

"I've never been there, but I've been told about it. You'll see. Apparently there are dancing girls … "

We crossed the Nile. The taxi dropped us off in Mohammed Square. The streets were deserted. We walked back up Kephren Street on foot. The shop windows were still lit up; some of the mannequins were wearing the veil too.

At a given moment we turned right, into a labyrinth of alleyways.

"Isn't there anything to fear at night?"

"No, not at all. In general, you're completely safe in Cairo. There are never any attacks."

"Well that's nice," said Martin.

At last we entered a sort of seedy bar whose name I have forgotten. A guy greeted us immediately and took us down into an even more worrying cellar. What awaited us was rather disappointing. Amplifiers were spitting out bad, distorted music. There was practically nobody there. But a woman was indeed dancing.

We were directed to a table at the back of the room.

"It's a bit average," diagnosed Jérémie.

We ordered three beers, which were brought to us immediately. As well as some pistachios in ample paper napkins. The dancing girl was a sort of veiled black pudding; we quickly turned our eyes away from her. On the other hand, one of the waitresses was quite pretty. She sat down between Martin and Jérémie. She didn't speak English and seemed completely indifferent to our presence: she confined herself to watching the dancing girl, doubtless her friend, and nonchalantly prepared the pistachios for us. Then she took it into her head to make us swallow them and placed them directly in our mouths in a way that was quite sensual, I have to admit. At last the dancing girl took a break. With silence re-established, despite the ringing in our ears, it was once again possible to talk.

"She's not bad, this waitress … "

She served us more beer with each mouthful, devouring us with her eyes.

"She's certainly pretty."

"But have you seen the way she's looking at us?"

"Anyway, since the beginning I've noticed that, in this country, the girls look at men very insistently … It's disturbing, you don't know what they want. In Europe, for example, the same look would mean: 'Come on, let's go upstairs, I want to go to bed with you!' So inevitably, when you're European, it throws you off balance … "

Martin was enjoying himself immensely, I think, in this role of the disappointed, fragile and sexually obsessed European. At one point, moving to the other side, the waitress placed her hand on Jérémie's thigh.

"Talk to her, you speak Arabic … "

"What would I say?"

"I don't know. Chat her up. Even if you've got no chance, it's interesting to see how she reacts."

The music started again, and a new dancing girl climbed onto what one might call, for want of a better word, the stage. At the side, Jérémie spoke into the waitress's ear. She laughed, but it seemed to me that this wasn't a good sign.

"What did you say to her?"

"I asked her if she wanted to go and have a drink with me, somewhere else … "

"And?"

"She simply said no, and left."

This was decidedly not the friendliest of bars. Jérémie shut himself in the toilets to try and phone Essam. He came back a moment later, victorious. We were meeting him in ten minutes. Thibault was supposed to be meeting up with us too. We swiftly finished our drinks and paid just before we went deaf.

Essam was the kind of guy who always turns up late, and in the wrong place—we could have waited for him for ever. The meeting was fixed for a square whose name I can't remember, not far from there. Martin explained to me that to his way of thinking, this was the best way of exploring a city: by visiting its basements and plumbing its depths. Another justification. Often, blokes came up to ask us if we needed any advice, since they could see us there, in the middle of a square, waiting for someone who might not come. I was quite surprised by their kindness, and above all by the climate of safety that held sway in this lost part of town.

"It's a very repressive system," said Jérémie. "There are cops on every street corner. So people have to behave themselves … "

And yet, two days before our arrival, a group of four tourists had been stabbed by extremists, just south of Cairo. One often heard it said, here and there, that the repressive system was the only form of government suited to the countries in this region; in any event, it was the only one that protected them from fundamentalism. Which would not have been the case with democracy. Egypt essentially made its living from the tourist business; so everything must be done to ensure a certain level of security, which is an absolute essential for tourism. In this respect, repression had one direct economic virtue: for the time being, it played a part in the country's development. Moreover, all the people who depended upon this business had an 'interested' relationship with the West and were not generally tempted by Muslim fundamentalism. But basically, I told myself, a dramatic decline in tourism would be sufficient for all these people to find themselves bereft and turn towards fanaticism. Hence the necessity for the fundamentalists to organise regular murderous attacks on tourists. Hence the necessity for the State to establish a strong power base.

Thibault had now joined us. He had apparently had dinner with a girl from the Embassy. Jérémie made another call to Essam. He'd be there any time now. And indeed a few minutes later, a white car stopped in front of us with a worrying amount of noise. Two guys got out; one of the two was Essam, wearing sunglasses. We shook hands. He looked at us a little haughtily, from behind his tinted lenses, as only saviours can allow themselves to do. Jérémie had a long conversation with him in Arabic. He was supposed to explain what we were looking for. What's more, what were we looking for? For my part, that had yet to be established. I remembered what Thibault had said the previous evening. According to him, Islam had succeeded in completely regulating social and sexual life. In fact, I was certain that sex was just as present as elsewhere, but that it was simply hidden. So all one had to do was ferret it out.

"You can search for ever," Thibault said again, "but you won't find anything in Cairo … "

Essam suggested we should get into his car. His pal looked a bit plastered, and it seemed more advisable for us to follow them in a taxi—a decision that we subsequently didn't regret.

"Right, where are we going now?" I asked, once we were in the taxi.

"They're taking us to a rather smart place, from what they've told me, a place where there's exactly what we're looking for … "

"And is it far?"

"It's on the Guizeh road, a quarter of an hour from here."

"Bloody hell, I'm supposed to go there tomorrow morning for the visit to the Pyramids!" Martin remembered. "I'm going to have to wake up early … "

I looked at my watch; it was almost half-past one.

"It's almost worth your while sleeping on the spot," I suggested.

The white car stopped at the side of the road. Essam got out and went into a café. He stayed there a while talking to another guy, all the time looking at us. We didn't know what was happening.

"Is this Essam one of your friends?" asked Martin.

"Yes, or at least, I know him slightly. I worked with his brother on a project for the Embassy … "

"So he's reliable … I mean, he's not leading us up the garden path?"

"No, no … I don't think so. Why?"

The white car set off again at top speed. I was beginning to have a bad sense of foreboding, as if some muffled threat were being slowly cooked up in the darkness. It seemed to me that we were about to enter another world. But I was curious.

Having said that, we were travelling a little too fast for my taste. I remembered that Martin had confided in me that he wasn't all that attached to life. I couldn't say the same. It wasn't my life that seemed to me to have some value or other, but life in general, the fact of being alive, which is sufficient to be afraid of death. Why were we going so fast? We weren't in a hurry. I was now having visions of an accident, and I was clinging on to the door handle for grim death. I could almost feel the sheet metal compressing us, reducing our four little existences to pulp, feel the twisted metal pierce our flesh and crush us, the blood in our eyes, and death. My parents.

Ten minutes later, the two cars parked at the side of the road in a cloud of dust. Essam pointed to the illuminated front of a sort of bar. As I understood it, we weren't in Cairo any more, but in the area around it.

"He says this is it," Jérémie explained to us. "But the admission charge is rather high … "

"That's fine, we've got our expenses!"

Martin looked drunk, and once again, as I saw the euphoria surge through him, I couldn't prevent myself laughing—but I think now that it was mostly a nervous laugh.

Essam told us to wait outside; he was going to see the owner first and discuss things with him. He came back a moment later and signalled to us to enter. He had a broad smile. What existed behind that frontage, shining at the side of the road? It seemed to me at that moment that it couldn't be anything murky, but after all, that was kind of what we were looking for: something murky.

Ten or so Arabs welcomed us with big, interested smiles. We were invited to go to the cash desk; it was four hundred Egyptian pounds per person. Martin insisted to Jérémie that we should be able to see what it was like before paying, but they wouldn't show us. So we had to pretend to leave so that they seized us by the arm and agreed to show us the 'big entertainments hall'—that's what they called it. And indeed, the name was well chosen: two girls, certainly decent-looking, were dancing to piercing music, but among the audience were around a hundred guys slumped in front of their beers, open-mouthed at a forbidden fantasy, that of barely-unveiled nudity—shoulders, arms, the navel, nothing more. They seemed completely hypnotised by this daring spectacle, as if they had sought to imprint as many images as possible in their minds so as to be able to recall them later and benefit from them more intimately until dawn.

"This is of no interest," Martin said immediately, manifestly disappointed.

Essam seemed vexed by his reaction; according to him, this was exactly what we had asked for.

"Not at all," answered Martin for the benefit of Jérémie, who was acting as translator. "This is like a provincial dance hall, we don't give a damn about it."

Essam got a bit annoyed. He wanted to know what exactly we were looking for.

"Tell him we would like to see what's behind the scenes … "

We found ourselves all at the side of the road, talking. Jérémie explained that Essam did not understand what was meant by 'behind the scenes'; we had to state things more clearly. The taxi driver was still with us. He had chosen to wait outside the bar to take us back to Cairo. He seemed pleased to see that we were already disposed to change our location.

"Tell him clearly that we are looking for girls," Martin finally let out. He was getting more and more determined.

Jérémie was horribly embarrassed. He didn't know how to get out of this, the words were almost unpronounceable for him, especially since Essam's brother was vaguely a professional contact, but I sensed that he was not against this idea of going on and seeing a little further. As for Thibault, he just kept repeating that there was no sex in Cairo. For my part I hung back, and I was finding this evening increasingly funny to observe: yes, basically it was a bit like Aragon and Drieu—but piteously deprived of their bordellos and their genius.

"He knows a place," Jérémie told us finally. "I think he has finally realised what we wanted … "

Ten minutes later, we parked outside a dilapidated hotel. What time must it be? The evening seemed never-ending, and this night would not lead to any dawn. The banner of Scheherazade was struggling painfully against total extinction.

"It's the name of the heroine in the *Thousand and One Nights*,"

Jérémie reminded us. "According to Essam, there's everything we want here, but if we're not happy, he knows a specialist bar just next door … "

In the lobby of the hotel, Essam talked for a moment with a white-haired guy. And I told myself that it was impossible to end up here if you didn't know the city; this was doubtless it, behind the scenes. We were asked to step inside a gigantic lift. What came next would take place on the seventh floor. As the doors closed on us, I realised that the taxi driver was still there, and that made me laugh. He had decided to follow us to the end of the night.

"It's a really funny atmosphere," Jérémie suddenly said, feverishly.

On the seventh floor, the doors opened onto a salon decorated in red velvet. There were several framed posters of women in kitsch colours. The man with the white hair explained to Jérémie how things worked. I was a little uneasy. As for Martin, he was standing in front of a small mirror, turning up his shirt collar.

"Right, let's find out what this is like … "

We had to follow another guy across a long corridor. Essam talked to his pal in Arabic. We were shown into a large room, which resembled a room for parties, or a large gymnasium, and again we suffered the same disappointment: a plump girl was dancing in front of inert, open-mouthed guys; as for the music, it was at such a saturation point that it was unbearable.

"This isn't true!" said Martin.

The white-haired man seemed to understand what was being said and spoke to Jérémie.

"He didn't know exactly what we were looking for," he explained. "But now he realises … There is another, more intimate place, on the floor above. He asks us to follow him."

So we crossed the corridor in the opposite direction. We

were indeed ready to walk kilometres so as not to prove Flaubert wrong … Then we were guided up a poorly lit staircase that seemed not at all designed for tourists, not even, to tell the truth, for the hotel's customers. "Come on, come on," repeated in English the white-haired man in a continuous loop, and I had the impression, I don't know why, that he was going to sell us his own daughters.

At last we reached the eighth floor, which was not at all like a hotel.

"This must be where the staff live," said Jérémie.

"That's what I was thinking."

"At last you're going to be able to find what you're looking for, Martin."

"As if I was the only one … "

"No! There's another one too," I said, pointing at the taxi driver, who was interminably there.

Jérémie gave an exaggerated laugh, which was an artificial way of putting a bit of distance between himself and the situation. But that laugh, once again, proved useless. The white-haired man, very pleased with himself, showed us into another room, smaller than that on the seventh floor, it is true, but inhabited by the same nightmare.

"This is really frustrating," said Martin.

Essam talked to us about the specialist bar he'd already mentioned. I was a bit tired, but we couldn't leave it at this. The white-haired man tried to keep us there by offering us drinks, but it was too late, we had taken our decision. To the delight of the driver, who was going to get back to his taxi.

"This doesn't have much to do with the *Thousand and One Nights*," noted Thibault perspicaciously. "But I did tell you: nowadays, Islam vows absolute hatred towards anything that approaches sensual pleasure … "

The driver set us down on a bridge, five minutes away.

Essam's car took a little while to rejoin us; they said they'd got lost. We thanked the driver; he could go home now. It was already three-thirty in the morning. He didn't want to go, but Jérémie insisted politely. The district was sordid. Undoubtedly very poor. I imagined dirty girls, with decaying teeth. We walked to the bar in question. Essam entered alone, and through the gap in the door I did indeed glimpse several girls. Essam's mate, who was decidedly uncommunicative, explained to Jérémie that we were supposed to stay outside while the negotiations took place: this was how things were done here. I then told myself that he knew this place very well. Why had he taken so much time to bring us here? I did not find an answer to this question, and the door of the bar opened.

We were seated around a low table. Five girls immediately came and surrounded us: they were all horrible and, so to speak, definitely unfit for the purpose. But we had thoroughly deserved it, after all. I almost wanted to laugh now. They gave us big over-made-up smiles, and clumsily attempted to make themselves seductive, which was tragically impossible. We were brought drinks. The cloth laid on the little table was stained. An impression of dirtiness exuded from the whole place. It was appallingly sordid. OK, we'd seen it, now we could leave. Not for a second did it occur to me that Jérémie or Martin could be interested in one of these girls. They weren't very young any more. And that made me think of the old bordellos, in France, as I was told about them, in any case. I'd been told several times how it went; about the women who initiated young men in a light-hearted, gentle and basically rather joyful atmosphere—in short, the opposite of current prostitution.

A girl sat down next to me. I had no desire whatsoever to

talk to her. I was ill at ease and pretended to be looking in the other direction. She asked me two or three questions in English, which I barely answered. My goal now consisted of finishing my drink as quickly as possible so I could extricate myself. Meanwhile, the girl, who doubtless wanted to get to know me better, took a handful of peanuts and attempted to put them in my mouth, which made me feel like a goose that somebody was hoping to force-feed. I had to fight her off. Seeing my resistance, she stuffed her hand sensually down her own gullet, without however ceasing to devour me with her eyes—I could tell from her eyes that this was a way of making herself even more desirable. I struck up a conversation with the person on my right, to get away from her, but Essam's mate wasn't very chatty, all the more so since he only spoke Arabic. Suddenly I felt alone. Just to accentuate my discomfort even more, another prostitute stood up and started dancing in front of us, then she attempted to take my hand and make me dance with her. She was so insistent that I had to get up and go and sit down on the other side of the table.

"Right, we're leaving soon, yeah?"

But Martin and Jérémie were deep in negotiations. A sixth girl, prettier than the others, and most especially younger, had sat down beside them. She was speaking to Jérémie in Arabic.

"Ask her if she'd agree to come with me to the Marriott," said Martin, losing no time in rejoining the discussion.

Jérémie did so and burst out laughing.

"What did she say to you?

"She said: 'What about you, don't you like me?'"

Martin wouldn't leave it alone.

"Why does she say that? It's got nothing to do with the question. What about me, doesn't she like me? Ask her why she says that."

But Jérémie was no longer listening. We had the impression

that he had entered into a real game of seduction and that he had forgotten whom he was dealing with. The two of them spoke in Arabic, completely omitting to translate for us. Martin then turned to me; his gaze was trembling with rage:

"What the hell's wrong with girls in this country? I'm disgusted … And you do realise this is the second time I've been given the brush-off by a whore … And look at the others: I'm bloody well not ending up with one of those ugly lumps!"

He looked really desperate; it was horrible to see. I even had the impression that he was going to start blubbering, and I thought back to the look in his eyes the previous evening, when we came out of the Egyptian Night. The other girls, noting that we weren't all that communicative, had now moved off. They were waiting, seated a few metres from us, in case one of us came to fetch them.

"Right, what are we doing?" I asked.

"I don't know. This really is the absolute end," commented Thibault.

"Are we maybe going back now?"

"You know what hurts me the most," Martin then said to me.

"What?"

"Telling myself that that girl, when she looks at me, feels exactly what I feel when I look at the other hags back there: disgust."

"No, come on … "

"And I'm going to tell you something: I think she's right to feel what she feels. In a way, it's what I feel too when I look at myself … Disgust. It's true. Have you seen my face?"

I couldn't find the words to answer him. It's true that he did look a bit like a frog. I wanted to leave now. And get out of here, away from this atrocious spectacle. The girl moved away for a moment.

"Right, what did you say to each other?"

"Nothing, we chatted … "

"Are you going to bring her back?"

"I don't know."

Jérémie was plainly very keen on the idea, but he was still embarrassed in front of us.

"Did you see how she ignored me?" Martin went on again, with a murderous look.

He didn't even answer.

"I'm a little hesitant."

"As you like, but make your mind up. We'd very much like to leave now."

The girl was already coming back towards us. Jérémie spoke at length with her. For my part, I attempted to signal to the waiter to bring me the bill. At last we stood up, soon to be liberated. Jérémie looked all worked up.

"Dammit! Do you know what she said to me?"

"No!"

"I asked her if she wanted to come with me."

"And?"

"She said we didn't know each other well enough … "

"Drop her! In any event, girls in this country don't fuck," said Thibault the expert.

"She told me: 'Not on the first night!' Like a young American girl … She suggested that we swap phone numbers and call each other tomorrow so we can go and get a bite to eat."

"But she's a whore, yes or no?"

"Yes. But here, whores don't fuck," Thibault concluded again.

Jérémie signalled to the girl one last time. They talked for another two minutes. No way of convincing her. From a distance I saw her shake her head. Martin was already halfway out of the bar.

"This is incomprehensible!"

"Yeah. It's really frustrating … "

"To say the least. It's like dying of thirst in the middle of the ocean … "

To everybody's surprise, the taxi driver was still there, outside the bar. He'd been waiting for us all this time. He looked delighted. In fact, out of everybody, he was the one who had had the best evening. Four trips in a few hours. We bade farewell to Essam and his mate who, rather sadly, told Jérémie that the girls we were looking for simply didn't exist in Egypt. And the taxi set off in the direction of the Marriott Hotel. During the entire journey, Martin didn't utter a single word. Twenty minutes later, as we were crossing the Nile on the Zamalek bridge, I realised that it was almost daylight.

7

EXPECTING THE WORST

I AWOKE LATE IN THE MORNING. It was too late to get breakfast. For want of anything else to do, I went and ran myself a bath, which ordinarily I never do (I mean in the morning), but that day I'd started out doing everything the wrong way round. What's more, I quickly forgot that the tap was running. I wrote a letter to Jeanne to tell her about the previous evening, and as I wrote, it was as if I was overcome by a malaise, a malaise I couldn't identify. I then stood up and went onto the balcony. A cloudy canopy weighed down upon the city. Then I remembered the bathroom: the water had seriously overflowed. I merely shrugged and turned off the tap.

Martin had gone off to visit the Pyramids. I wasn't unhappy to find myself alone. I was vaguely planning to walk through Islamic Cairo, to visit a few mosques, lose myself in the city, forget about myself a little. When I got out of the bath, I gave Jeanne a call. I felt the need to tell her I loved her. I got her answering machine. I left her a message. People often reiterate that you shouldn't say these kinds of things, and that when feelings are expressed simply and straightforwardly, they contain a sort of ridiculous gravity, which is in bad taste, to the point of being unforgivably vulgar and in the end counter-productive. And this rule apparently doesn't just apply to feelings of love, but to any form of impulse towards the other person. At the extreme, the only way of expressing something is simultaneously to instil intentional doubts about the sincerity of what is being said. I had for example noticed that people quite rarely abandon the falsely detached, ironic attitude that protects them so well from the world. Everything that is expressed nowadays can only be done so through the distorting filter of slight distance and humour—not real humour, but jokes, derision, the stuff of fleshless jibes. Everything has become a pretext for laughter, but for stupid, coarse laughter. One set of people distanced from the others, that is to say, basically, one set at the expense of the others. A person who thinks and feels for himself can never participate in the world's joyless euphoria. It is this which signals the end of conversation between people and therefore, in a certain way, the reign of loneliness.

I got dressed while I thought about all this. I took a little money from the safe, checking at the same time that my plane ticket was still there, and closed the door behind me. I went down to reception to ask them to post my two letters and confirm my flight for the following day. Then I went into the garden. The sun had returned, so I sat at a table and I ordered a coffee. I stayed there for some time, abandoning myself to a gentle torpor. I could hear voices coming from the swimming pool, from the distance, and the sounds of people diving in. In this semi-somnolence, I experienced a sensation of well-being which, little by little, wiped away the feeling of unease I had woken up with. A new day was beginning.

A little later, a taxi took me into the centre of Cairo. I walked through the souk in the hope I might disappear into the shadow of its alleyways, yes, forget myself, but the different sellers constantly brought me back to myself, by attempting to palm off their wares on me. I went to the al-Azhar mosque, one of the world's pantheons of Koranic knowledge. It seemed to me that I could see unreasoning hatred in several people's eyes, pure, abstract, infinite hatred, whereas up to that point I had had the feeling of a profound kindness. However I did what I could to remain discreet. Not like that guy next to me who filmed everything that happened with his camcorder, compulsively, without thinking about what he was seeing, or more exactly without thinking about what he could no longer see—his eyes blinded by the rabid desire to bring back something of his journey that would survive. I thought of my brother. During the different journeys we'd made as a family, he had always taken on this job: filming. And I told myself that this tourist was as far removed from the reality he wanted to capture as my brother had always been from us. Isolated, the pair of them; forever more isolated.

After the death of our parents, he had taken a faintly obsessive interest in pictures depicting car accidents. He said it was a photographic experiment. "César had built up quite a collection of crushed cars, so why not pictures of accidents?" he said to me, obstinately rejecting the link with our own story. He talked about mounting an exhibition one day. To all outward appearances, there was no commitment in what he was doing, he didn't give a damn about road safety—just this devastated metalwork, the shattered windows, these crushed shapes, ravaged by the impact, the brutal halting of movement that had taken the name of freedom, all this seemed profoundly aesthetic to him. Each time when he showed me his work, although I could not fault him I felt an immense unease, stupidly seeking among the smoking wreckage the charred remains of my mother, and the anxious smile she would have given him if she'd seen him so lost.

Then, in October of the same year, as if some evil destiny had been set in motion, my brother in turn had an accident: nothing very serious fortunately, but because of an injury to his knee, he had to go for physiotherapy, and over several days spent a lot of time with people who had had serious accidents, survivors who were frequently missing a leg, an arm, often more, and who were nevertheless continuing to live. This sight profoundly upset him, and changed him too I think. Several times he told me he couldn't complain any more. He had finally found the images of horror that he could relate to his own pain. He no longer needed his photos. At the same moment, he abandoned his plans for an exhibition.

As I walked through the streets of Cairo, I was confronted by something rather like that sense of relativisation. Suddenly the reasons for our incessant complaints became groundless. A series of indecent whims.

After a while, I returned to the Marriott where the Embassy's car was waiting for us. It would soon be time for the last talk. I was ripped off by the taxi driver but basically that was unimportant. It was the taxpayer's money. I even gave him an extravagant tip.

Mathilde was already in the car. She seemed relieved to see me and asked me if I knew where Martin was.

"I think he went to visit the Pyramids this morning. But he ought to be back by now."

"Well no, actually … "

"Isn't he in his room?"

She had attempted to call him several times: nobody had replied. We decided to wait a bit. Doubtless he wouldn't be long.

"It was good last night, wasn't it?"

"You mean, the dinner?"

"Yeah … "

I was astonished: on the contrary, it had seemed to me that she had been profoundly bored.

"So what did you do afterwards?" she asked me again, more from the fear of silence, I think, than from real curiosity.

"We went round some bars. Nothing very exciting, I'm afraid."

"But there's nothing going on here at night, I've noticed that. It's a country where everything happens in the daytime."

She was perhaps not wrong. But I couldn't find anything to say by way of reply. She was now compulsively looking at her watch. We couldn't be late for the talk, she kept saying. She went off for a moment to attempt to call Martin again. I smoked a cigarette while I waited. I wanted to go back to Paris.

Mathilde came back. She looked anxious: Martin still wasn't answering. I wanted to reassure her:

"Perhaps he's gone directly to the reception … He had no reason to go back to the hotel, after all."

"You think so?"

"I'd imagine so, in view of the time."

She remained pensive for a moment. I had never looked at her up to that point. She wasn't very beautiful, it's true, but the seriousness with which she did her utmost not to be late had something quite touching about it. She wanted to be up to the task that had been entrusted to her. She must be one of those fragile girls who fight all their lives to exist, to get people to look at them a little, despite their ugliness, so as not to disappear completely into insignificance.

Time was moving on. We decided to leave without Martin. During the journey, I made the mistake of asking her one or two questions—which was sufficient to make her pour out everything I hadn't asked her, her life in its entirety. I gave her a fixed smile, nevertheless conceding the odd 'yes, of course' from time to time, so that she could retain the illusion that she was being listened to. But I felt that soon her words were going to completely swamp me. I was already short on air. She related her grandmother's illness as well as listing the psychological (and therefore necessarily subtle) reasons why she couldn't bear being late.

It seemed to me then that everything she might say had in reality just one purpose: to make people desire her, feebly admittedly, somewhat out of pity, but desire her nonetheless. Yes, it seemed to me that Mathilde had a desperate need to be taken, here or elsewhere, to be caressed and thus emerge from the non-existence in which she had been placed by this insipid quality which, when you came down to it, characterised her more than anything else.

"So, are you with anyone?" I asked her in the middle of her monologue.

She smiled awkwardly, caught unawares by this phrase, which sounded like an attempt at seduction, and she rearranged a lock of her russet hair a little nervously.

"Sorry?"

"I mean, are you living with someone?"

"No. Not at the moment … "

"How's that?"

I asked her this rather to please her, for basically I knew very well how it was.

"There's nobody I'm all that interested in, that's all," she said without conviction. "And besides, we're in Egypt … "

All the same, there were quite a few Frenchmen at the Embassy. Fifty maybe. But doubtless she preferred to remain alone than to sleep with someone she wasn't really in love with—in any event, that's how she had to describe her enforced single state. And in the meantime, life was passing her by.

"What about Jérémie?"

"Oh, no! Jérémie's a friend, nothing more … "

My first thought was: "In any event, it wouldn't exactly be a gift for him … " Then I thought back to our bar-crawl the previous evening. After all, the girl with the green eyes he had wanted to bring back with him wasn't all that much prettier than Mathilde. So why wasn't he interested in her? The answer was obvious. To have a hope of getting off with Mathilde, he would no doubt have had to take her out to dinner, tell her she was pretty, funny, elegant, that what she said was really interesting—in short, lead her progressively to believe that this was about more than just a desire to fuck her. If that happened, she might refuse to have sex on the first night. As if desire itself, this desire that deep within herself she sincerely craved, constituted an attempt on her person. What did we take her for? If she wasn't with any man, it was first and foremost because she had decided not to be, because she didn't give herself to the first guy who came along, and because 'nobody interested her all that much'. Yes, she would doubtless have refused; but after all, the girl with the green eyes had also refused.

I didn't want to ask her any more questions about this. The situation would swiftly become embarrassing. Anyway, I could easily imagine what this poor girl Mathilde's daily life was like. And I told myself, rightly or wrongly, that life was really unjust since she was probably more capable of love and generosity than any other girl.

Again I thought back to our trawl round the bars the previous evening. Basically, the thing that had left the biggest impression on me was not so much the absence of sex as the obstinacy with which we had sought it right to the very end of the night. I remembered what Martin had said on emerging from the last bar, in the small hours: he had talked of 'frustration', thus implying, if one took account of the discussion we'd had with Thibault, that it was Islam which, through its formidable morality and hatred of sex, was perversely eager to maintain this feeling. And yet, as I thought back over it, it was most of all his own attitude that had struck me, his frantic quest, his frenzy and finally his despair, and I told myself that the frustration he had spoken of was above all his own, that is to say independent of the precise circumstances of our evening out, and that he must cart it around with him permanently. It is, I believe, one of the painful paradoxes of the West: the exacerbation of frustration despite so-called sexual freedom.

After centuries of frigidity, quite relative for that matter, the West had freed itself little by little from its religious morality and its social prudishness. It is generally considered that this is a good thing. From a certain point of view, however, the increase in sexual encounters that has arisen as a result has been a veritable 'human catastrophe', whose most obvious sign is the dissolution of the last barricades protecting the individual from the market society, in other words the married couple and, to a lesser degree, the family. But the most astonishing thing is that this progressive liberation has not enabled individuals, as one might have thought, to emerge from frustration. On the contrary it has placed before them the spectacle of their own powerlessness to respond to the growth of their desires—as I understood it, this was the theme of Martin's novels.

I then thought back to the look in his eyes, two days before, when we came out of the Egyptian Night and the two girls had given him the brush-off: I had clearly seen a sort of hatred, not aimed at them in particular, as I have already said, but at the whole of humanity. And that same look, coming out of the bar at dawn: an assassin's look. At that moment, I was convinced that he could have launched himself into a career as a murderer without any problems. If Martin had, through his writing, encountered a degree of notoriety, this was essentially because he had contributed, along with others, to defining the new market society into which the West had entered, in order to transform itself progressively into an area in which all human relations responded to the demands of newness, attractiveness and profitability. This configuration concerned all human relations without exception; as for Martin, he had essentially taken an interest in their sexual dimension. On the market, each individual, perpetually hoping for erotic encounters, had its own and in the end quite objective value. Indeed, within a system of transactions, we're dealing with an exchange rate. His wasn't very high, in his own eyes at least. This was doubtless what he'd wanted to tell me, in that bar, the previous evening, when he had talked to me emotionally about the disgust he felt for himself.

In a more general way, the criteria of differentiation corresponded roughly to the models first peddled by porn, then by the feminine press, and finally by advertising. For both sexes, attention was essentially directed towards age, size, weight and salary. Evidently the physical criteria alone were not sufficient to determine an individual's erotic destiny. It's obvious that other elements were also added, among them money, social position, sense of humour … From that point, the competition was violent and bitter. The two girls' rejection, in the garden of the Egyptian Night, then rejection by that other girl in that dodgy bar, who had preferred Jérémie to him, was like the echo of all the rejections he must have come up against in a market society. Except that those girls, because they were paid, theoretically ought not to have expressed a preference. It is this silence, as much as access to the body, which the client buys. Doubtless this is why Martin was so attracted by prostitution: in the end it is the sole area spared by competition.

And yet, in the bar, the girl with the green eyes really had said to Jérémie, out of disdain for Martin: "And what about you, don't you like me?"

After this trip to Egypt, in view of the rather extraordinary events that were to take place, I reread all of Martin's books. In his second novel, the principal character goes constantly from one woman to another. Rather unpleasant, without any real characteristics, he is almost exclusively driven by this multiple, unstable and therefore essentially fleeting desire; you could even say that his vision of the world is limited to it. In his mind, the lack of personality (recognised as a general tendency of the modern individual) was intimately linked to the outpouring of desire appropriate in any advertising-driven society. By dint of desiring everything (in response to the stimuli imposed from the outside), the modern individual came to stop desiring anything at all any more—or in any event, to stop desiring anything personally, and therefore, in a certain way, to forsake individual existence. In this respect, the characters in his novel had primarily the appearance of ghosts with no substance, driven by the permanent hope of sexual encounters. Nothing more.

"Have you ever read Martin's books?" I asked Mathilde as we approached Heliopolis.

"I've read one."

"And?"

"That was enough for me."

What he recounted must have been too raw for her. Or rather, she must find the truths he attempted to approach too painful, too dangerous. And to protect herself, she must force herself to find it vulgar. It was a classic case.

"I didn't like it that much … "

She must prefer books that are eager not to say anything at all, and which hope to redeem themselves by engaging in a purely stylistic quest behind which reality fatally slips away.

She gave me a rather bizarre little smile. We were on slippery ground. Since the first day, moreover, Mathilde's face had seemed familiar to me, and several times I had asked myself if I hadn't seen her somewhere before. Yes, really, her face seemed familiar to me. That little smile for example. But it was only at that moment that I realised where this impression had come from. In fact, Mathilde looked like a girl who'd been at high school with me, in the lower or upper sixth, I can't remember which. I took a little while to remember her name: she was called Astrid Grégoire.

Astrid wasn't very pretty either. I think you might even say, without risk of exaggeration, that she was frankly hideous. At the time I knew her, her face was covered with a layer of red, granular tissue, and her teeth, unlike her, were particularly spoilt. What's more—and this didn't help matters—she was slightly simple. All this was enough to isolate her from the world and annihilated any hope of being loved by a boy one day. For the same reasons, she had no friends in the class. Nobody ever spoke to her. But this was doubtless not the first year of loneliness for her. I even think she must have always been the girl people could hardly remember and whose sea-monster face they noted in passing. A profound indifference reigned around her, and there was no reason to hope that it would one day be otherwise. Certain lives pass by like that, in silence. She arrived in the morning and didn't say a word until evening. Basically, now that I think back, I might even have doubts about whether she really existed.

Obviously I don't remember the day I saw her for the first time. All I'm saying is that she was in my class. She worked hard but wasn't a good student. But she hung on. Doubtless she already knew she would have to fight harder than the rest in order to succeed. But for what purpose? What did she dream of achieving? At the time, I didn't ask myself many questions about her. Like everyone else, I accepted her presence while feeling a little sorry for her, but not too sorry, and above all, at a distance.

I began to take an interest in her, following an insignificant incident. One day, between two lessons, I went to the toilets, and as I was washing my hands, I heard someone sobbing behind a door. I approached, and almost said something. There was no doubt: it was a girl. And yet we were in a place reserved for boys. But what surprised me more than anything was the terrible intensity of her sobs. If it is possible, this person was physically dying of distress. I didn't know what to do. In the end I went out, without making a sound. In the corridor, I encountered a guy and started talking to him. It wasn't premeditated, but by so doing, I was able to see Astrid emerge discreetly from the toilets a moment later. So it was her. For the next hour, I was seated a few metres away from her and I observed her: there was no longer any trace of those sobs on her face. Her eyes seemed as dry as usual. And I told myself that this might not be the first time she had locked herself away like that to weep. I even told myself that she must cry like that every day. Amid general indifference. Certain lives also pass by like that.

A few days later, coming out of school, I followed her down the street. At first it wasn't intentional, we were simply going in the same direction, then my curiosity took the upper hand, and at the point when I ought to have turned right, I continued along rue Saint-André. The weather was pretty good that day. I'd guess it was sometime in May. She walked as far as the boulevard. Then she went to have an ice cream in a brasserie. She watched the passers-by through the window. She had the look of a little girl, seated by her window. I don't know why, but at that point I told myself there must be stuffed toys in her bedroom. From time to time she must embrace them forcefully. Basically, she was condemned to watch the others flying the nest without uttering a word: bodies discovered pleasure, relationships were forged, the girls put on make-up, the boys chatted them up continually, and she … she was eating an ice cream in a lonely brasserie.

This went on for quite a while. Then she stood up and left. Even today, that is still the perfect image of loneliness to me: Astrid Grégoire sadly eating an ice cream while watching through the window as the people pass by.

8

A LITTLE DEEPER INTO UNEASE

L AMIA WAS WAITING for us. Martin wasn't there yet. Someone rang the hotel again, but in vain. He was quite simply impossible to find. Since time was pressing, the woman co-ordinator decided to start without him. All the same I was a little anxious, and I suggested to Mathilde that she should call the guide who'd taken him to visit the Pyramids, to check that nothing had happened to them. While the co-ordinator was speaking, I thought back to my uncle and aunt: if that was the case, a camel-driver must have tried to abduct Martin …

There wasn't much of any interest in the debate. Banal comments fired off, one after the other. When my turn came, in a rather hesitant voice I just quoted a comment made by Husserl, in the mid-Thirties, about the crisis in European humanity. He saw the roots of this crisis (so deep that the phenomenologist even wondered if Europe would survive it), in the beginning of modern times, that is at the moment after Descartes and Galileo, when science had begun to reduce the world to a simple object of technical exploration. According to him, it was from that point onwards that man, launched into specialised disciplines of knowledge, began little by little to lose sight of himself, to the extent that he sank into what Husserl's disciple Heidegger called 'the oblivion of being'.

In one of his books, Kundera returned to this analysis, adding a most important correction. According to him, there was a close link between the roots of this crisis and the European art of the novel (the qualifier 'European' designating not a geographical entity, but a spiritual identity born with ancient Greek philosophy and which one might ultimately associate with the word 'western'). Because for Kundera, the founder of modern times was not only Descartes, it was also Cervantes:

"If it is true that philosophy and the sciences have forgotten man's being, it seems all the more evident that with Cervantes a great European art was formed, which is none other than the exploration of this forgotten being."

In other words, the precise raison d'être of the novel is to protect us from this oblivion of being by maintaining life in a perpetual blaze of light. Thus, the art of the novel is a positive deduction from a malaise beginning with modern times. Expressed in this way, one could better understand the terms of the problem: if the Islamic world generally had difficulties with the novel, it was because it was living to a large extent in an era that belonged to the period before modern times, bogged down in archaisms that were by their essence incompatible with the foundations of the novel: freedom, fantasy, complexity, the ambiguity of all truths and the suspension of moral judgement. In this respect, the novel could easily become the battle ground between two civilisations.

This was the best response I could make to what had been said about *Madame Bovary*. I do not know how accurately the translator re-transcribed my words, but, as I finished my last sentence, I sensed a new atmosphere of aggression in the hall.

After the talk, Mathilde caught me by the arm and told me that the pyramids guide hadn't seen Martin that morning: he hadn't turned up at their meeting place. He had disappeared, and we had no means of getting in touch with him.

"But where can he be?"

"I've no idea ... "

All of a sudden I had a bad premonition. But I was the only one worried. I sensed that Jérémie was more inclined to think he had willingly cut himself off.

"He's useless ... It's just not the done thing, not turning up ... "

"Perhaps he had a problem, or something."

"No ... "

"Perhaps we should ask someone from the hotel to go and look in his room, don't you think?"

"What for? If there'd been a problem, they'd have realised, what with the chambermaids and all that ... "

He was very optimistic. I imagined Martin's body in the room. Naked in the bathroom for example. He was in the middle of having a shower, very early that morning, after two hours' sleep, and suddenly something happens, and his body falls like a dead weight, there's a muffled sound, his head has struck the edge of the bath, his jaw has shattered, and very quickly a lake of blood forms. A few hours before, he had taken care to hang a little sign on his door asking not to be disturbed, and the body was still waiting—I recalled my own bathroom, that same morning, when I'd left the water running and it overflowed—only with blood on the floor. Red. Or in his bed, sensibly asleep, a death in pyjamas that had occurred during his short sleep, without explanation, just like that, a bolt from the blue. These things could happen any time. It's not at all unlikely. When you thought about it, it was even the most likely scenario.

I insisted that we return to the hotel as quickly as possible. There was a pseudo-cocktail party with the cultural attaché and the organisers of the book event, and I was supposed to remain there. I asked Jérémie if it wasn't possible to leave earlier than planned. He replied that it was difficult. "As regards the attaché ... " And besides, there was no car available. I pretended to understand. I went off to wash my hands, and left by the rear door. There was bound to be a taxi somewhere. But I happened upon Lamia in the street, talking on the telephone on the opposite pavement. She signalled to me to wait for her, then hung up.

"What are you doing?"

I didn't know what answer to give.

"Listen, I think I'm going to take a look over at the hotel … "

"Look for Martin? Doesn't anyone know where he is yet?"

"No. And you see, I'd rather check."

"But we've already tried calling his room. There's no point in going to the hotel … and besides, there's the cocktail party you know."

"Yes, I know."

She remained silent for a moment.

"Are you going to take a taxi?"

"I'll get by."

"If you want, I'll take you … "

"You've got a car?"

"Yes."

It was parked a minute away. I almost felt like running. I realised that my impulsive behaviour was a little excessive, but I couldn't do anything about it. Once again I saw his murderous look from the night before. I didn't know that he might be its first victim.

"You look completely freaked out!"

"How long is it going to take at this time of day?"

"With the traffic jams? At least half an hour."

"Hell, you feel so stupid when you haven't got a mobile … "

Lamia put on some music, which enabled us to remain silent for quite a while. Little by little I became aware of the point-lessness of what I was doing. If nobody answered the door in

Martin's room, I didn't know what I was hoping for. In fact I found myself rather ridiculous, and had the impression that I wasn't the only one in the front of that car who thought so.

The streets were jammed solid. We hardly moved forward at all; it was really unbearable. I wondered how people could live in this city. And it was while I was wondering this that I wondered whether Martin had left Cairo. Yes, after all, he might just have left. I could quite easily see him taking an earlier plane than planned. A sudden impulse. To return to France. I thought about his anger the previous evening, his mad rage. Or maybe he'd left the city. Gone south, towards the women of Nubia. Following our misadventure, he might have taken the decision to go there. Naked women. To take his vengeance on something ungraspable. Martin would have been capable of that. I also thought back to the tourists who had been stabbed by extremists a few days before our arrival. All these things could explain his absence. I could already imagine him stone-dead at the side of a deserted road.

"You look really worried," Lamia said to me calmly.

"No, no, I'm OK … "

"The jams aren't as bad as I expected. We'll be there in twenty minutes at the most."

" … "

"Do you know Martin well?"

"I'd never set eyes on him before this trip … But don't you find it worrying, the fact that nobody's seen him since last night?"

"No … you know, if something had happened to him, we'd already know. News travels fast in Cairo, especially about foreigners."

Then, with a disarming smile, she told me that I mustn't immediately imagine there'd been a catastrophe. According to her this was a characteristic attitude of Westerners; she called it 'the fascination of evil'. In all probability, Martin simply hadn't digested what we'd eaten the previous evening and couldn't move more than ten metres away from the toilet! It was quite common, according to her. I listened to her attentively. I know perfectly well that she was right. I often had a tendency to exaggerate. I would have liked to explain to her that I was burdened with a new seriousness since the death of my parents, an awful lucidity about the extreme fragility of life. I would have liked to tell her about my sleepless nights, my irrational fears. I would have liked to tell her how this handicap forbade me to have any hope of peace: I got myself into completely excessive states as soon as I couldn't contact Jeanne by phone, for example; I strove to express the solemnity of a farewell each time I said goodbye to someone; I was forever constructing catastrophic scenarios from completely anodyne elements: a delay, an absence, a look that was a touch too melancholy. I could have explained all of this to her. But I chose to remain silent. And yet, without anything being said, it seemed to me that she understood what was happening inside me. I had the feeling that my body had become transparent, and that she suddenly had access to everything I was keeping to myself; I was naked, unadorned, and her eyes seemed to say to me: "Don't worry, everything will be OK, it'll all work out in the end … "

When we arrived outside the hotel, she offered to accompany me, but I refused. I remembered that she had her dinner with Cotté at the Embassy. I thanked her for bringing me this far. She waved me off. Immediately I went up to the seventh floor. I was with a Saudi family in the lift: the two children, their eyes lowered, the veiled wife, and finally the man, whom I had seen two days previously with a twenty-year-old prostitute in the casino bar. Once I was upstairs, I went and knocked on Martin's door. We had adjoining rooms. Nobody answered. Again I visualised his body stretched out in the bathroom, and told myself that I couldn't go on doing nothing. I almost went to ask at reception for the master key. But I chose to go into my room. The balconies might be connected. I opened the sliding glass door. I leant out sideways in an attempt to see into his room, but the sun's reflection turned it into an opaque screen. I've always suffered from vertigo. Only about a metre separated the rails of our respective balconies. So I could move from one to the other without taking too many risks. What's the ground speed of a body that falls from the seventh floor? Once I reached the other side this was a pointless question. I placed my hands on the glazed door to try and see inside. The room was empty. But suddenly the bathroom door opened, and Martin appeared. I felt a profound sense of relief. He was naked, in his socks and sunglasses. I was a bit embarrassed to knock just at that moment. It might be better if I went back via my room. So I was just about to leave his balcony when he opened the door.

"What the hell are you doing there?"

"Me? I … I was looking for you."

"I'm here," he replied, still just as naked.

We both realised this at the same time. He went back into his room to fetch a towel and put it round his waist.

"We've been looking for you all day … "

"I know."

"What happened to you?"

"Nothing. I wanted to be alone, that's all." His face was sombre.

"Has something happened to you?"

"No, I told you. I didn't wake up this morning. And afterwards, I didn't want to see anybody … Did the talk go well?"

"People asked what the fuck you were playing at."

"If you fancy a drink, go ahead, help yourself from the minibar … "

He went into the bathroom to finish getting dressed. He came back without his sunglasses. He had a black eye. I didn't say anything to him. Then he realised he'd forgotten his glasses. He rushed off into the bathroom. I went to get a fruit juice from his bar to hide my astonishment. What had happened? Who'd he been fighting? I told myself straight away that he hadn't gone off to bed that morning, after the last bar. He might have gone back down after saying goodnight to me. To the casino, for example. Or elsewhere.

"Where are the others?" he asked me.

"Still at the book event. There was a cocktail party … We'll see them shortly. Jérémie's reserved a restaurant for this evening."

"Count me out, thanks."

"Why?"

"I've told you, I want to be alone."

"Is it because of last night that you're like this?"

He just shrugged his shoulders.

"We've all got our theories," I said again to relax the atmosphere. "I wondered if you'd gone back on the plane. But Lamia thought the dinner had disagreed with you and you'd spent the whole day on the bog … "

"What a silly bitch she is."

I couldn't understand his attitude.

"Are you sure everything's all right?"

"All I can tell you is that this is the last time I'm ever setting foot in this shitty country!"

"If the only aim of your journey was to meet girls, you should have gone to Morocco, that's for sure … "

I offered him a cigarette. He accepted. We went back onto the balcony to smoke. The sun was already low. We stayed there for quite a while gazing at the city. From his balcony, unlike mine, you could see the Nile. I don't know why, but that river has always made me dream.

"In any case, you can't really understand," he told me finally.

"Understand what?"

He gazed into the distance, towards the Cairo Tower, which reached up into the sky.

"Goddammit, you saw my face … "

It was terrible; I couldn't even tell him he was exaggerating.

"And what's more, before, I was fat as well! At least in that respect things are a bit better now … "

I managed a faint smile. I couldn't find anything to say in reply. From that point on, he started talking to me about his past. This lasted a long time. Maybe half an hour. Throughout this time, I didn't interrupt him once. I looked at the Nile. And it was as if it was telling me everything that was going to happen that same evening. He talked to me essentially about his adolescence. Later, reading his novels, I realised that he had already written down a lot of what he told me that day, on the balcony of that hotel, but that he still hadn't recovered from these first wounds.

Everything begins on the banks of Lake Geneva. He lives in a little village whose governing ethos is the 'Vaudois spirit'. For those who don't know, the Vaudois spirit is made up of the very worst in hypocrisy, meanness and collective stupidity. By way of an example, it is in the mountains that the famous Swiss cuckoo clock was invented; since then, nothing of any note has happened. For him, adolescence could be summarised as a succession of humiliations. He has the misfortune to be thirteen years old, too fat and too short. What's more, quite quickly he senses that he will be condemned to the painful observation of other people's pleasure. At secondary

107

school, the boys start to go out with the girls. Rumours of sex are already circulating in the corridors. But all these things will not be for him. It has to be said that he is an accumulation of all the world's defects: ugly, bad at sport, timid, with a bit of a yellow streak and no fashion sense. Just as his childhood is clearly reaching its end, without any alternative mode of existence having yet presented itself to him as a viable possibility, he realises that he is in effect, and above all sexually, under a sort of death sentence.

Things get worse at high school. He looks at his fat body in the mirror, and he sometimes wants to die because of what he sees. Deprived of friends, he turns in on himself. And then a slow process of self-destruction begins. Around him he observes the others, with silent hatred, as they form couples without too much difficulty, observes the chatting-up sessions at evening events, the break-ups that are talked about, happy life, tittle-tattle about performance—all of this profoundly sickens him. At this time, his capacity for illusion is still intact, and he still dreams of love. He even thinks he has encountered it towards the end of his time at school. She's called Vanessa. She's quite beautiful and, even beyond his hopes, she likes him quite a lot; which is sufficient for everything to be shattered in a single blow.

They both live in the heights of Vevey and take the same bus to get to school. For several months, Martin silently observes her. The day she says hello to him for the first time, he has already undressed her a thousand times in his imagination. The following year, they find themselves in the same class. When she is ill, he's the one she calls to catch up on her lessons. Overnight he becomes a good student. At this time Vanessa is going out with an idiot whom Martin regularly dreams of leading to a slow, painful death. Towards the end of the year, something happens. She is absent for several days on the run and no longer answers the telephone. A little anxious, Martin goes directly to her house to check that nothing serious has happened. She invites him in. She tells him that she's unhappy and has split up with her bloke. Martin listens. From that point, they become close friends. Doubtless Martin doesn't frighten her. She tells herself that a fat boy isn't a very threatening thing for a young girl. He often comes to her home, at the end of the day. They chat. One evening, their discussion goes on longer than usual. Vanessa's parents aren't there. She invites him to stay for dinner. She even opens a bottle of wine. Throughout the dinner, Martin has a massive erection; he doesn't help her to clear the table.

Then they settle themselves in the living room. For the first time, he talks a little about himself. He takes the risk of disappointing her. But Vanessa looks at him with shining eyes: if only all boys were as kind and deep as he is, she tells herself. She is touched by what he's telling her. He doesn't know what he ought to do. The situation is beyond his hopes. She is so beautiful. He almost wishes he could die so as not to spoil anything. It is late now. She is very close to him. You're shy, she tells him at one point. He wonders how he should interpret this phrase. He brushes her hand. She responds with a troubled smile. His heart howls, and the entire world capsizes into pure irrationality. He dares move closer to her. His simmering life hangs upon this precise moment. She too leans a little towards him, and their lips touch. This is it, he tells himself at last. This is it. He almost faints. How long did that kiss last? Doubtless a scant few seconds. But for Martin it is like the entrance into another world, the enchanted vase without the magic potion.

Suddenly she recoils. She stands up. She regains her awareness of reality. She apologises: "I'm sorry, I don't know what came over me!" Martin doesn't know what to say. Why is she apologising like this? She puts her hand in front of her mouth, dazed, as if she's having difficulty realising what has just happened. "No problem," he replies awkwardly. She has a desire to laugh. To laugh at the situation, which in effect means laughing at him. In a moment, Martin once again becomes the chubby boy he detests being. And she says again: "I'm really sorry ... At the moment I'm just doing silly things ... I don't know what came over me ... Excuse me ... " She's trying so hard to stifle her abominable laugh that she can't finish her sentences. Life is not exempt from cruelty.

Martin is a silent witness at his own execution. He makes a modest attempt to convince her, but to convince her of what? She replies that he must go now. And that he must forgive her. It's a nervous laugh, she says. He has difficulty swallowing his saliva. It's one of the last times he will see her, he can sense that already. From now on she won't answer the telephone when he calls. She will avoid him at school until the summer holidays. She will be ashamed. He has to leave. Vanessa becomes impatient. Now he's the one who's apologising. He goes to fetch his jacket. And the door closes behind him.

"And you've never seen her again, since then?"

"Yes. Once ... "

"And?"

He gave me a sad smile. I realised that he preferred not to talk about it; evidently it hadn't been any more pleasant.

"Afterwards, I went to live in Paris with my mother. We lived in the north, by the La Fourche Metro station, do you know it? An unsavoury area. It was then that I lost weight. All of a sudden. For no reason. It didn't make me that much more alluring, but fine, it was one complex less. In any case, I didn't try anything with girls. I was too afraid that they'd laugh in my face, do you see what I mean? I knew perfectly well that it would always be like that for me. Unless I did something a little exceptional. It's at that moment, I think, that I decided to become famous, but I didn't yet know how … For several years, I swear to you, I detested life. It was only when I started writing, years later, that I felt a little more at peace."

For a long time I said nothing. I sensed that his suffering was immense. Gaping wounds. In a certain way, he would always be that adolescent deprived of love—his sickness was incurable. In one of his novels, the main character, who gives himself the nickname of Jean-Foutre la Bite, haunts the streets of Paris, metro trains, and public parks in search of a woman. Sometimes he walks close to the outer boulevards where, at night, girls wait for men to come and pick them up. He observes them from a distance and, the rare times anyone hails him, his heart skips a beat and he walks faster, as if he had not heard anything. Still too shy to answer their calls. This story, which at first I had found a bit insubstantial and unpleasant, now seemed to me to be completely desperate, and beautiful. At that time, he must have been eighteen. In the story, he ended up having his virginity taken by a girl from rue de Saint-Denis.

I don't really know why Martin told me all this, at that precise moment, but it seems to me that it was in order to relate it to everything that had happened over the last two days. In the garden of the Egyptian Night and especially in that bar at dawn, it was still Vanessa's laugh he had heard, and that was just unbearable to him. I understood better now the frenzy with which he talked about 'naked women'. It was as if he wanted to stifle that evil laughter.

"What about Mathilde?"

I don't quite know how I came to ask him that, but I think it was from that point on that the discussion resumed a normal course.

"What about Mathilde?"

"What do you make of her?"

111

"She's not great."

Then, with an ironic smile, he added: "It'd certainly be in her interests to convert to Islam … "

"What?"

"I mean she's got the sort of face for radio. Like me. Why?"

"Oh, nothing."

"Has she said something to you?"

He seemed faintly intrigued. I had been clumsy. Basically I had just wanted to bring him back to the present, make him talk about something other than his humiliations. Now he thought that Mathilde had said something specific to me about him. Which was untrue. But I couldn't see myself telling him so. I was effectively compelled to advance towards a different truth, perfectly constructed and designed to reduce a little the suffering to which he had made me a party.

"Oh no, nothing … But I got the impression she liked you a lot. She said so during the day. Frankly, I think she really fancies you … "

"Oh?"

At that moment, I had no idea of the consequences of what I had just said. So it was in all innocence, I believe, that I lied to him. However, I cannot prevent myself feeling responsible for what subsequently took place.

9

PARADISE

I WENT DOWN TO JOIN JÉRÉMIE. The restaurant he'd had in mind was closed. He suggested that we dine at his place. He would order in some *mezzes* from a trader in his district. I remained very vague on the subject of Martin. He had felt a bit unwell, dizzy … But he was better, and would no doubt come and have dinner with us. That is what I confined myself to saying.

"Who else will be there?"

"I don't really know. Thibault may join us."

"And Mathilde?"

"Yeah, she'll come, I think. On the other hand, it'd amaze me if Lamia came … "

"She's going to the Embassy with Cotté."

"Really? Bloody hell, she never stops! She only arrived a few months ago, and already she's attending official dinners … "

"Well yes, what can you do? You have to get used to it, women are more cunning than you."

After that I spent quite a while in my room, reading. Then I got dressed before going to fetch Martin. Still in his dark glasses. He looked to be in a better mood. But I could sense that he was a little embarrassed in front of me. Doubtless he blamed himself for having told me too much. Confidences are always admissions of weakness. What's more, in the lift he reproached me for never talking about myself.

"There's nothing particularly interesting to say."

"More likely it suits you to get other people to talk. It's more comfortable."

"Not always ... Are you keeping your glasses on this evening?"

"Yes."

"It's more comfortable ... "

"Not only that ... "

We picked up a taxi opposite the hotel. Jérémie lived on the other bank of the river. His building was very old, its lift cage completely dilapidated. You had the feeling you were in a dodgy area.

"This gives you confidence," commented Martin. "When you know that apartment buildings fall down with impunity in Cairo ... "

Jérémie had the entire first floor to himself. It was a big apartment with high ceilings and wide open spaces.

"Here you are!" was his only comment on our arrival.

In the central room, an immense bookcase climbed up the wall, and I was surprised to see that he had brought all his books from France. I walked round the apartment. There was a guest room. And, in the sitting room, a baby grand piano.

"I bought it when I arrived. It's not very good, but it's pleasant to play from time to time."

"Aren't the others here yet?"

"They'll be here soon."

Martin sat down at the piano. I thought I recognised a piece by Debussy. The alcohol was placed on the low tables, and Jérémie poured us each a glass. We drank to Egypt, but our hearts weren't really in it.

"Don't you want to go back to France, after all this time?" I asked him.

"That depends on the day."

"I don't know how you can live here," cut in Martin, continuing to play his piece.

"Oh, I adore this country. I'm more at ease here than at home. In fact, the nearer the date of my departure gets, the more nostalgic I am. It's a bit stupid, but that's how it is: I'm nostalgic about this country before I've even left it … "

"You know, I think my problem is that I detest Islam," Martin went on. "Frankly, I detest it. I know it's not something people are supposed to say, but it's true."

"Why?"

Jérémie seemed more and more irritated by Martin.

Somebody knocked. It was Thibault. He had a bottle of vodka with him. Plus a smile that arrived at just the wrong moment. He asked Martin why he was wearing sunglasses, but received no reply. I went to the kitchen to fetch some ice, so as to serve it very cold. When I came back into the sitting room, I halted in front of the bookcase and inspected Jérémie's books for a moment. Notably they included Flaubert's *Correspondence* in the Pléiade edition, and I told myself that it had been following us everywhere since the beginning of this trip—or that, on the other hand, we had been constantly following it. It was like a recurrent motif. I opened it at random. A scrap of paper fell to the floor. I picked it up. A sentence was written on it, in black ink, no doubt in Jérémie's handwriting. "A good writer is one who takes us precisely where we don't want to go." It was typical of the sort of daft phrases I can't stand. I closed the volume, put it on the shelf with the other Pléiade editions, and went to sit down with the others.

"It's really not bad here, in your place … "

"Thank you."

"You certainly couldn't have a place like this in Paris," added Thibault.

He gave us a rather exhaustive list of the disadvantages of

having an apartment in Paris. I was quite surprised to note the extent to which one person's ideas and those of the others resembled each other. Basically, each person wanted roughly to live in the same place. The criteria were almost identical. But after all, this observation was not limited to housing: in the majority of fields, the people shared the same criteria for appreciation, pleasure and comfort. One must have an excessively strong capacity for resistance today in order to manage not to sacrifice everything to the ravages of identicalism. For example, Thibault, in terms of quality of life, alluded to the fantasy of the little village. He attributed a mad charm to some street or other simply because there was a market there once a week. "It's really nice … It makes it a bit like a village … Everyone knows everyone else … " he said.

"And why don't you just go directly to the country and live there?"

Somebody else rang the doorbell at just the right moment. Jérémie went to let them in. It was Mathilde, but she wasn't alone: Lamia was with her.

Martin's piano playing stopped dead.

"Well! We thought you were going to the Embassy!"

Poor Mathilde: nobody commented on her arrival. Lamia was wearing a black dress that left her shoulders bare.

"I didn't really feel like it. I'm not disturbing you, am I?"

"No … quite the opposite."

From a distance, Lamia gave me a smile. I no longer knew what to think of her. Deep down, she was rather surprising. Martin got up from the piano and poured himself a drink.

"So! We've been looking for you all day … Are you feeling better?"

"I'm fine, I'm fine," he replied in a dull voice.

Jérémie put some music on and went into the kitchen to fetch out the different dishes he'd had delivered an hour previously. Mathilde went with him. Martin's eyes followed her.

She was wearing a rather bizarre maroon-coloured dress. It wasn't a foregone conclusion.

Thibault and Lamia were talking about a girl from the Embassy whom I didn't know. I joined Jérémie in the kitchen. You could sense that he didn't eat at home very often: he searched in all the drawers to find where the plates were stored. Mathilde looked at me in an odd sort of way.

"The cultural attaché wasn't too annoyed with me for leaving without telling him, was he?"

She looked a bit annoyed. She shrugged her shoulders.

"Really, I thought it was best to check that everything was OK with Martin … It seemed more important to me, do you understand?"

"So, what was the matter with him then?"

"He wasn't well. Nothing serious … "

Jérémie looked at me with amusement. Doubtless he thought I was trying to chat her up. He left the kitchen and—I didn't realise until later—commented on his impressions in front of the others: "That one doesn't waste time in the kitchen … " It seemed to me that this was the moment to talk to her a bit about Martin, to prepare the ground.

"He was a bit sad, that's all. We talked a little … I find him really touching … "

"Touching?"

"Yeah, really … "

"That's a strange thing to say. Because if there's one word I can't see associated with that guy, it's that one."

"Oh?"

Yes, distinctly not a foregone conclusion. At this, Mathilde carried the dishes into the living room. I followed her and felt all eyes turn towards us, or rather against us, and notably those of Martin, mingled with irony, malevolence and sadness.

Thibault, who clearly had an idea about everything, had embarked on a long monologue. He had been trained as an economist and often referred back to theoretical systems that were a bit too simplistic. He said that, for the first time in history, western societies were confronted with problems no longer of penury, but of over-abundance. "Almost all sectors of activity are suffering from over-capacity. There are so many cars that we're beginning to run out of space to drive them! We have so much to eat that we're experiencing epidemics of obesity! There are so many things to see, read and do that you can't find the time to take advantage of them all! In fact, there's too much of everything! It's the major symptom of the West ... "

Everybody started helping themselves from the different dishes placed on the big table. Martin stood a little to one side and tapped dreamily on the piano as he searched through the sheet music.

"There are too many cars in Cairo too," cut in Jérémie.

I got my hands on two glasses and poured drinks for Lamia and Mathilde.

"Ah! The ladies' man!" exclaimed Martin wearily.

I realised he thought I was trying to seduce Mathilde, and that moment I decided not to look at her again throughout that evening. I even smiled at Lamia.

Quite quickly, the discussion stopped being collective, and groups formed. Thibault was left with just Jérémie to converse with, and I forced myself to talk to Lamia so that Mathilde would feel a little lonely. At one point she finally stood up and approached the piano.

"Can you play?" she asked Martin.

"A little. But not that well ... "

There was something profoundly immodest about his excessively artificial modesty.

"Is that why you're wearing sunglasses?"

Martin gave her an embarrassed smile. What's more, she had a crap sense of humour.

"What about you, do you play?"

"Oh no, not me. I had a few lessons, like almost everybody does, but I gave up a long time ago … I was tormented by a crazy teacher."

"Yes, like almost everybody … "

From where I was seated, eating aubergine caviar, I could observe Martin. He had become charming again with her. Deep down, he had an astonishing personality, quite ungraspable. I couldn't decide if I liked him or loathed him. He was now saying something in her ear, and I almost had the impression that I hadn't completely failed in my efforts. Why couldn't two such lonely people come together? Now there's a massive question.

As for Lamia, she seemed to me to be a lot less sure of herself than I had expected. She talked to me about politics, in particular, no doubt seeking to soften the judgement I might have made of her. She brought up the vanity of it all. Often, she had to fight inside herself a feeling of 'what's the use' that devoured her from the inside. I could quite see what she was talking about.

Thibault then suggested going and joining some of his friends after dinner, but nobody seemed that interested and besides, dinner wasn't finished yet. Lamia got up and went off somewhere for a moment.

"Do you realise what you're doing there?"

It was Thibault, invariably smiling, who asked that question.

"Me?"

"Yes, you. The two of us have been working on Lamia for six months! And you come along and chat her up right under our noses!"

"I'm not chatting her up. I'm talking to her."

"It's the same thing."

Mathilde stepped away from the piano and went to rejoin Lamia.

"Still, we're better off here than in all the bars of Cairo, eh?" asked Thibault again, with an enthusiasm that was frankly beginning to get on my nerves. Martin started playing the piano again until the two girls reappeared. It was a piece by Keith Jarrett. He stopped playing when Mathilde came back into the room; they continued their discussion in whispers. I poured myself another glass to celebrate my small success as a go-between, but the vodka had already lost its coolness. I returned to the kitchen to fetch some ice. I'd already drunk a bit too much.

At one point—was it much later?—Martin came over to see me.

"Listen, I've got something to ask you … "

"What?"

He signalled to me to follow; Thibault was a few metres away from us.

"Have you heard the latest one?" he asked us.

"No," replied Martin, leaving the kitchen without waiting for the reply.

He went directly to the guest room. The light was off. Through the window, the moon gave the foot of the bed a pearly glow. Martin pressed his forehead to the glass.

"What's the matter?"

"I need you to do something for me … "

"Is this to do with Mathilde?"

"No," he replied with a disturbing smile. "It's to do with Lamia."

"What now?"

I was on the point of going back into the sitting room.

"I have to explain to you … Do you fancy her or not?"

"Why?"

"Tell me if you fancy her … "

I sensed that he was going to tell me something strange, but I was very far from imagining just how strange.

"I think she's pretty, yes, why?"

"Are you going to try and fuck her tonight?"

"Bloody hell, stop asking all these questions!"

"It's important."

"No. I am not going to try and fuck her!"

I was thinking of Jeanne. And in the end it was very good that he had forced me to say this so clearly to myself.

"Then I can ask you to do this thing for me."

He remained silent for a moment, and I had the impression that he was doing so with the sole intention of maintaining an insubstantial air of mystery. He took out his cigarettes, offered me one, lit one for himself, and finally began explaining to me what he was on about.

"There's something I didn't tell you back there … "

I thought of his black eye, and indeed he removed his sunglasses.

"Last night, when you'd gone to bed, I went out again … "

"Yes, I'd worked that out."

"I took another taxi. I went back to the bar. The last bar, you know. When I arrived there, you could tell it was soon going to be light. I don't know, it must have been around six am. They were closing up. But all the same they let me in. They must have told themselves I'd left something behind inside. One of them spoke English. An old guy who was counting up his cash at the till. He poured me one last drink. The girls weren't there any more. I asked the guy if they'd already gone home. He replied that it was late. As he said so, he pointed upwards, as if he was indicating the upper floor. Then I asked him if they lived here, upstairs. He said yes, as if that was obvious. Not all of them, but two girls. I finished my drink. I stood up. Somebody showed me where the toilets were. It was even grottier in there than it was in the main bar. I went to wash my hands."

"OK, cut to the chase … "

"As I looked at myself in the mirror, I no longer understood what the fuck I was doing there. But I knew that everything could topple over into chaos at any moment. I came out of the toilets, and went up the little staircase. After this, there was a sort of long corridor with different doors. I realised that I was here to find the girl with the green eyes again. To have my revenge."

"What are you on about?"

"I opened the first door. It was the sitting room. But almost empty. I went on. I walked along the corridor and went into one of the bedrooms without making a sound. There was a bed there, and in the bed there was a girl. It was her. I could do whatever I wanted. She was a few metres away from me."

"And … "

"How can I put this? All at once, I realised I was acting crazy. It wasn't her I wanted revenge on. It wasn't her, it was Vanessa … Do you remember, the girl in Switzerland?"

"Yes, yes … "

"So I didn't do anything. At the same moment, she turned over in bed, saw me, cried out, seconds later a guy charged in, and here's the result," he said, putting his dark glasses back on.

"You got yourself punched … What are you on about? Do you really expect me to swallow that?"

Suddenly Jérémie switched on the light in the bedroom.

"What the fuck are you doing? Is there a problem?"

"No, no … We were just talking, but we're coming."

Jérémie seemed rather irritated. He closed the door again behind him and left us alone.

"There's something else I have to talk to you about," Martin went on. "When I told you that story, in Switzerland, you asked me if I'd ever seen Vanessa since then, do you remember? Right. I told you yes, but I didn't explain where or how. Well, I'm going to explain it to you now. In fact, the girl Vanessa I told you about is the girl you know as Lamia ... It's as simple as that."

I didn't believe him. He realised that from the look on my face.

"Lamia means Vanessa in Moroccan."

"I don't believe you."

"As you like."

"But you've known this for a long time? Is that why you came to Egypt?"

He gave me an evil smile.

"No, that's not why ... I didn't realise until this morning. Up till then, I had doubts. It was practically ten years ago. She's changed quite a bit. But this morning, I had the confirmation ... "

"How?"

"It's complicated."

Doubtless it was linked to his disappearance.

"And what about her, does she know?" I asked finally.

"No, I don't think so. But that's quite understandable. I've changed a lot too. Before, I was fat and had an adolescent's face ... And above all, Martin Millet isn't my real name. It's the name I took to write my books ... So no, she can't know."

I no longer knew what to think.

"But she's never lived in Lausanne! She told me she came from Paris ... You're really talking rubbish!"

"It's true. She says she was born in France and has always lived in Paris, but she's lying."

"Why would she lie?"

123

"I don't know why, but I swear to you that she's lying ... "

"And what about you, why are you telling me this?"

"I told you, I need to ask you to do something for me. But it's delicate ... "

"You want to take revenge, is that it?"

He remained silent for a long while and drew on his cigarette, visibly edgy. He searched for his words as if he feared how I would react. I was edgy too: I think I had already worked out his machinations.

"What I would have liked to do is seduce her. But that's impossible. She hasn't given me a single glance since I arrived in Cairo. I'm under no illusions: I don't exist for her. I can't fuck her. But you can."

"How do you know I can?"

"I've done some digging. I know she likes you a lot. She talked to Mathilde about it just before."

It was at that moment that I realised he had been engineering everything since the beginning of the evening. I thought back to his whisperings with Mathilde. Once again I saw Mathilde joining Lamia in the kitchen ... All at once I felt stupid, with my attempts at little arrangements. I hadn't understood anything of what had been played out before my eyes.

"The problem," he continued, "is that I can't get my revenge alone ... I mean, I can't get myself into a bedroom with her. Whereas you can. You can get her up to your room. So you can get her up to mine ... Do you understand?"

"Are you kidding me?"

There was a diabolic smile upon his face. Then suddenly it relaxed:

"Of course I'm kidding you ... "

"Bloody hell, you're a nutcase. I'm not finding this funny."

After that, the talking continued in the sitting room as if nothing were amiss. Martin had adopted a different face, and it seemed to me from time to time that he had almost forgotten what he'd said to me. He spoke only to Mathilde. I heard him laugh several times. For my part, I remained silent, troubled. I wanted to go back to the hotel, but I couldn't see myself leaving Martin here. After all, I didn't know what he was capable of. In a way I was supervising him. It was around one o'clock in the morning that the tensions started to return.

Lamia was explaining that to Egyptians, she had an accent that enabled them to identify her Moroccan origins immediately. Consequently they were more tolerant and left her a little more in peace …

"And yet," Martin then said to her in a very calm voice, "in Morocco they are also completely crazy when it comes to women, aren't they?"

From the way he was talking, you could sense that he'd drunk far too much.

"That depends. Anyway, in every … "

"In those parts an emancipated woman is regarded as a prostitute, isn't she?"

"That depends by whom, I'm telling you."

"I have a very close female friend who went off to live in Tangier for a few months for her work," he explained, still just as softly. "She told me how things went, and it's not at all the way you think it is when you go there once from time to time, say to Marrakesh for a holiday … First, she told me that there are only men in the streets, the cafés, the restaurants. The women didn't have the right to go out … "

"Yes, but that's cultural … "

"All at once, all these guys became aggressive as soon as they saw a western woman walking in the street. They had the impression she was trying to provoke them. For them, a woman walking down a street on her own is in itself a form of provocation … "

"Surely not!" said Mathilde, who knew nothing about it.

"You know what that friend told me? At each street corner, guys looked at her with mad aggression. The look of a rapist. And they called her a 'Christian whore'! That's how it is: a Frenchwoman walks alone in the streets of Tangier, and she's called a 'Christian whore'!"

"In Tangier, that's true," agreed Lamia.

"Basically, the truth is that all these guys desire her. That's the sole problem, I believe. They see a girl whom they associate with the western system (i.e. in general terms, with freedom of behaviour) and they dream of being able to possess her at the same time as forcing themselves to despise the system she represents. And as they can't possess her, this little Frenchwoman in the streets of Tangier—mainly because they haven't the right, because of Islam—they begin to detest her!"

"What do you mean?"

"I mean that the hatred they express when confronted by the woman is in reality an impossible form of desire. That's what I believe. And it's very understandable! Imagine, when you're eighteen years old, in those parts, you can't yet marry because you don't have any money, there are no emancipated girls, and prostitution is expensive … Imagine the state of frustration! Islam is a gigantic exercise in frustration! It's like here, in Egypt. In fact, the entire city is a giant erection! An erection without end!"

"An erection that's slipped out of hand!" quipped Thibault, who took a while to recover from his own joke.

"That's where the hatred of women derives from: frustration. That's all I meant to say, but perhaps I'm wrong."

Doubtless I was the only one who detected the dual meaning of what he said. I tried to change the subject of the conversation, but in vain.

"You say it is because of Islam," Lamia went on. "But you're wrong. It's simply culture that's the cause … Take me, for example. I'm French, of Moroccan parentage, I'm a Muslim, and everything's fine. I'm not frustrated and I don't detest anybody … "

"Do you really say your five prayers a day?"

"No, but I practise in my own way."

"So you're not really a Muslim."

"What? What are you saying?"

I grabbed the packet of cigarettes lying on the table. I lit myself one.

"You're a Muslim in the same way that I'm a Christian. In France, for example, the majority of people say they're Catholics, but they aren't really. They're cast-offs of Catholicism. They're Catholics in terms of racial origin and culture, if you like. But they're not really Catholics. Being a Catholic doesn't just mean being baptised and believing vaguely in God; it implies a certain way of life. And it's the same thing with you; you don't really apply the Koran. You've adapted it to your view of life, you've retained what interested you, you've put aside what you didn't like, in short you've gone shopping, but you've moved away to the point where you're no longer a real Muslim."

"Oh yes? And what is a real Muslim?" she demanded, brows knitting.

"A real Muslim is someone who applies the precepts of the Koran. Not just those that suit him or her, but all of them. It's not a criticism! For me, you see, Christianity becomes beautiful when you detach yourself from it. And in the same way, Islam has never been so intelligent and amiable as when it leaves only a trace in the life of an individual … In any case," he continued, topping up the glasses with vodka, "there is a practical incompatibility between the Western system and Islam, I'm sure of it now, and this incompatibility will become more and more obvious to each of us."

127

"You're going too far," I said then. "And you're wrong."

Lamia remained silent a moment, to think.

"Your problem, you see, is that you don't take account of any nuances ... "

"What nuances?"

"For example, it doesn't even enter your head to distinguish moderate Islam from extreme Islam ... "

"Yes, that is indeed the subtle distinction everybody is constantly making everywhere. You can't read a page of a newspaper without being reminded of it: it is right, but it doesn't solve the problem. Very often, nuances are a way of not thinking. And I think we should be a little more wary of them. In France, the art of the nuance has completely stifled any possibility of considered thinking. It has become practically impossible, for example, to utter certain words without being immediately suspected of having wanted to utter others. And of having silenced them. One is obliged to keep silent. There is an obligatory silence on all these subjects ... First of all it's been repeated to us continually for months that we above all mustn't confuse Muslims with Islamic fundamentalists, which is the least of things, I'll grant you that. But this determination not to confuse problems has ended up creating general confusion, which is just as worrying. Anyone who thinks in depth about Islam, for example, is immediately suspected of wanting to say different things from what he or she actually says. For example, anyone who puts a finger on the aggression and instinct for domination that are undeniably part and parcel of this religion is immediately accused of having in fact wished to criticise the Arabs. In fact, a superior kind of confusion has developed in public opinion, one you can't go back on and which is similar to intellectual terrorism. In this context Voltaire, a part of whose work aimed to drive out loathsome things from the Catholic religion, its superstition, its essential fanaticism and its extravagance, would have had to leave France—moreover, that's what he did!"

"But what are you getting at?"

"When I say that for me, there's an incompatibility between Islam and the western system, I don't need to take refuge behind a distinction between moderates and fanatics, since I'm talking about the religion, about the way in which it explains the world. There's this egalitarian fervour and this cult of tolerance, which would have us believe that all values are worth the same. But nothing could be more untrue. And for me, the values of Islam are sometimes dangerous and regressive, that's all. In France, a large number of Muslims are like you: they say they're Muslims, but will never pose problems of incompatibility because they have moved a long way from their religion, most of the time without completely realising it. But I'm talking about the kind of Islam that doesn't make compromises with the real world. Just one example: a guy who must say his five prayers per day cannot be integrated into the western system, it's absolutely impossible."

"You're wrong. But I'm going to say this to you: it doesn't surprise me that you don't like nuances, because that's precisely what you lack. You haven't a single nuance, not a hint of finesse."

"What I don't understand," cut in Thibault, to soften the discussion a little, "is why Islam is so strict about sex."

"For a long time, Christianity was even more strict," said Lamia, as if to defend herself.

"That's clear," added Mathilde, who was trying to participate in the discussion.

"Except that Christianity said people mustn't enjoy themselves now, so as to save their souls, whereas the Koran forbids enjoying yourself now so that you can enjoy yourself later, which isn't entirely the same thing ... "

"How do you mean?"

I sensed at this moment that Martin was about to say something unpleasant.

"For the most part, Muslim countries are in absolute denial about sex. I didn't know that it was so hard, but you've already told us so yourself: here, the frustration is immense, you can see it in everybody's eyes. Now, you know what martyrs are promised, for example?"

"No … "

"In paradise, a martyr is a hero, but above all, and this is no mean thing, he is entitled to seventy-two virgins all to himself. That's important, I think, in order to understand terrorism a little better. All these young guys are incredibly frustrated: it's normal that they should not remain indifferent to such propositions … "

"Are you saying that for you, suicide bombers' motivation is sexual?" asked Mathilde, her brow furrowing in a faintly disdainful manner.

Jérémie had got up to go and play the piano. Lamia joined him almost immediately, refusing to pursue the discussion.

"Partly. But I'm going to put it to you in a different way: if I was a Palestinian, for example, if I had nothing, no wealth, no real future, had lost several members of my family in the war and, above all, it was impossible for me to sleep with girls, that is to say if I was in a system of maximum frustration, frankly, if somebody suggested I should go and blow myself up in the midst of the enemy and I'd instantly find myself with all those women to myself, yes, frankly I don't think I'd hesitate for a single second … I'd go and blow myself up at the French Embassy!"

"What you're saying is a bit too simple."

Mathilde was now looking at him with disdain. She was manifestly disappointed by what she was hearing.

"Yes, it's simple … But things aren't necessarily very complicated. It's simple. Very simple, even. But it's true! And it's precisely so as not to be confronted with this truth that everyone is so eager to make us believe that the problem is very complicated! Engineer a good dose of sexual liberation in these countries, and that'll be the end of terrorism!"

Jérémie began a piano piece with the obvious intention of drowning out this unpleasant discussion.

"There's one thing I don't agree with," Thibault said finally. "In France for example, before sexual liberation, people were also very frustrated, right, well, all the same they didn't go and blow themselves up."

"Yes, but the western state of frustration has never equalled that of the Muslim world. Fifty years ago, it was easy to have a mistress … And prostitution was rife. Basically, the only moment of comparable frustration was the age of the great crusades. Absolute chastity. You can see what that caused: it was quite simply unbearable for them to know that people were fornicating in other countries. So they went off religiously to war, violating countless young Muslim girls on their way, just as the Algerian pseudo-holy war has brought about thousands of rapes in ten years! This is what I'm saying: Jihad, like all holy wars, has one principal motivation, sex."

"That's not stupid," commented Thibault, stupidly.

"You're saying that because you didn't manage to chat up a single girl last night," retorted Jérémie from the piano. "That's all."

Everybody was tired and the mood was quite disgusting. It was time to go back. I went off for a moment to have a piss. And when I came back, Martin was on the floor, completely drunk. We laid him out on the sofa. Jérémie looked annoyed. He was afraid we'd decide to leave him there all night. Lamia had a car. She agreed to help me bring him back to the hotel. It was risky for her car seats. We carried him to the car, and put him in the back. Thibault lived in the vicinity. However, Mathilde came with us. Her apartment was on the way to the Marriott.

Nobody spoke during the journey. In the rear-view mirror I could see Martin, head back, mouth open, and Mathilde, who was looking at him with profound disgust: so this was how this final evening was ending. I remembered the idea I'd had a little earlier to set things up between the two of them. And I couldn't prevent myself from laughing.

"What's up?" Lamia asked me.

"Nothing. Actually I find all of this very funny. For me, the pathetic and the dramatic always verge on the comic … "

She gave me a smile. I don't think she really understood what I meant.

"How is he?"

"He's stopped moving."

When we arrived at her place, Mathilde just gave us a wave of the hand by way of goodbye. That gesture embodied all the weariness in the world. Then she disappeared behind a heavy wooden door. She seemed sickened. I then thought again of Astrid Grégoire and, without quite knowing why, I imagined Mathilde alone in her apartment, sobbing.

Then we crossed the Nile. The streets of the city were deserted. Once we were outside the hotel, we wondered how to proceed. It was a bit embarrassing to arrive via the main entrance, carrying Martin. Lamia suggested going through the back entrance. She parked the car in the hotel car park. I picked up Martin and followed her in the darkness. A guard briefly searched us and let us pass. We went through the entire hotel like that. Then we took the lift. All three of us. I thought back to what he'd said in the guest room, at Jérémie's place. In a way, the situation was quite curious. I almost had the impression that I was carrying out his plan: we would soon find ourselves in his room. For a moment, I wondered if Martin was really asleep or if he was still manipulating us. I shook him, but he was like a dead man.

The key to his room was in his jacket. The door opened without difficulty. Then we put him on his bed. My back was wrecked.

"What happened to him?" asked Lamia.

On the way, we'd lost his sunglasses. The area all round his eye was purple.

"Hm? He must have banged his head … "

"You reckon?"

I confined myself to a shrug of the shoulders. To tell the truth, I lacked too many pieces of the jigsaw to make out what had really happened. I was rather tending to the belief that he'd told me a load of old rubbish, but I couldn't say any more than that. Lamia went over to the minibar.

"Do you think I could take something? I'm parched … "

"Yeah, of course."

She opened a guava juice and sat on the sofa. The curtains weren't drawn, and in the darkness the sliding glass door was like a big mirror. I took a fruit juice from the minibar too. I wasn't thirsty though. I sat down opposite Lamia. She gave me an awkward smile.

"This is a bit of a bizarre situation."

I agreed with her. Especially in view of what Martin had told me. I knew he was sleeping deeply there, five metres away from us, but I couldn't prevent myself feeling that he was listening to us and that a part of my freedom had been taken away from me. I suggested to her that we should go and finish our fruit juices in my room. We closed Martin's door behind us, and went and sat on the sofa in my sitting room.

"It was a funny sort of evening, wasn't it?"

"Yeah, a bit. Even a bit unpleasant, in certain respects … "

"Perhaps … "

Now we no longer knew what to say to each other. She

smiled the whole time. She was really pretty. We were at the other end of the world. Both of us. In a hotel room. Tomorrow, I would return by plane to Paris. Everything was in place for me to lean towards her and kiss her. But there was Jeanne. I must keep to what I had told myself: I would not kiss Lamia.

I wanted to get her to talk about herself, but she didn't talk much. Basically, I realised, it was no longer the time to talk about one's past, one's childhood and all that. It was time to kiss or go to bed. She was waiting. She was waiting for me to make a move on her. For me to lean towards her.

"Are you tired?" she asked me.

"I'm OK … How about you?"

Once again she gave me an ambiguous smile.

"No. Not really."

I couldn't make up my mind. And yet it was simple, all I had to do was tell her: "Right, it's time for you to go now … " And instead of that, when she asked me if I was tired, I answered that I was OK. Things weren't OK at all, in fact.

"It's funny, isn't it, the two of us finding ourselves here … "

"Funny?"

"Unexpected, I mean."

"Why?" I asked in a voice that had almost faded into nothing.

"I don't know. I wouldn't have believed … "

I thought back to what Martin had told me. That would help me to resist. Not kiss her. Then, without any transition, I asked her if she'd ever been to Switzerland.

"Switzerland?"

She laughed. It's true that it had come rather suddenly …

"No, never. Why?"

"No reason."

"Ah."

We'd finished our juice. She laughed a little about the

situation. She must think me timid. And yet that wasn't entirely the case. I was simply struggling with all my contradictions. I no longer even asked myself if Martin had been wrong about Lamia or if he had lied to me. For the moment, my sole problem was myself, or that part of myself which wanted to stretch out a hand to her.

"What are you thinking about?"

"Hm? Nothing."

"Come here," she said to me then, very softly.

She laid her hand on my shoulder and kissed me. I was a prisoner. I now had a sort of obsession with seeing her breasts and, without moving away from her mouth, I tried to work out how her dress opened. But suddenly, as if gripped by horror, that cold monster which held possession of my belly and which I had grown accustomed to calling 'my love for Jeanne' reared up, and I recoiled. This was not what I had told myself. I could still decide what happened to me.

"What's the matter?"

"I can't. Sorry."

"What?"

"It's nothing to do with you. I've drunk too much … "

"Huh?"

"And I love a woman in Paris."

In a flash, I saw scorn appear in her eyes.

"You've remembered that a bit late, haven't you?"

"I've told you, I'm sorry."

She attempted once more to kiss me, but I turned my head away. Then she opened up the top of her bodice to hound me into a corner. Her two breasts appeared. She closed her eyes. I didn't.

"Come on, who cares … "

"You have to leave," I told her with a sad smile, realising that I was precisely carrying out what Martin had asked me to do: pushing her away.

She didn't understand. I stood up to give added weight to what I was saying, and it was at that moment, I think, that I noticed, behind the sliding glass door which, in the darkness, had transformed itself into a sort of opaque mirror, the unobtrusive silhouette of Martin. He was there, on the balcony, watching us. Just for a second, I had seen his gaze turned towards us. Lamia asked me what was wrong. I rushed to the sliding door and opened it: there was nobody there.

"What the hell are you doing?" she asked me again.

Without answering her, I strode across the gap between our two balconies. I realised that Martin had been manipulating me from the start. Had he really watched us? Or had that been just a hallucination? The glazed door of his room was open. Yet I remembered closing it when we left. Now I had to enter his room and, without quite knowing why, I was afraid—I saw myself again as a child, at night, in the interminable corridor of the apartment, singing the Marseillaise to myself to give myself courage and forcing a way through to the bogs. Afraid, for Martin was no longer on the bed. The light was on in the bathroom, but it was empty. He had disappeared. What was he playing at? He'd probably gone out through the door. Perhaps he had knocked at the door of my room. Lamia, thinking it was me, would have opened it, and he would have found himself alone again with her in my room—exactly as he had told me that he wanted to do it. All of this passed through my head in an instant. I was trapped, but at the same time this trap seemed impossible to me, unreal and confused. I rushed out onto the balcony. I strode over the gap in the opposite direction. And I came nose to nose with Martin. He was closing the sliding door from the inside. I just had time to stick my arm through the gap. Lamia was huddled up on the sofa. I was able to open the sliding door. Martin didn't do much to stop me. He was wearing his diabolic smile. He also had something in his hand, a glass perhaps, but I didn't have time to see it, I threw myself upon him. At the first punch, he fell to the ground. It was perhaps only at that moment, now that I think back, that he got his black eye. Yes, I was probably the one who injured his face.

Lamia didn't really understand what had happened. She had got dressed again. I think she had been afraid. She looked at Martin on the floor and said: "When I think that he was saying just before that it was the Muslims who became violent because of frustration … You really are two pathetic guys!" Then she left without turning back. It was better that way. And I found myself alone again with Martin. I don't know why, but I thought then that I was going to start crying. A spasm rose up inside me, a sort of disgust for all of this, and I could already divine its violent, irrational intensity. I hid my face in my hands, in the hope of holding myself in. I closed my eyes. I stayed for just a short moment like that, not moving, waiting for the tears. But nothing came. I was going to calm down. Then suddenly I felt my whole body contract; I bit the inside of my cheek, but in vain; and I felt the spasm overcome my resistance, rise up my throat, a volcanic eruption, and burst out in an unpleasant, frightening noise. I didn't understand straight away.

It took me a few moments to realise that I was laughing.

10

THE FASCINATION OF EVIL

NEXT DAY, Jérémie came to take us to the airport. It must have been around ten o'clock in the morning. The sky was veiled by a thick mass of cloud. Neither Lamia nor Mathilde came to say goodbye to us. I was in a hurry to get back to Paris. In the car, we remained silent. Martin kept his eyes closed. He must have had a headache. Nothing in particular happened until we checked in our luggage. Jérémie said a limp goodbye. It was rather sad to part like that.

During the flight, Martin didn't speak to me. By chance, we weren't really next to each other: an aisle separated our two seats. What exactly did he remember? When the hostess came by to serve refreshments, I heard Martin ask for a guava juice. I don't know if this was an allusion to the previous evening or simply a coincidence. As there wasn't any, he had an apple juice. After that, I may have fallen asleep. I don't really remember. At Roissy, we lost sight of each other in the arrivals hall. I didn't even see him disappear into the crowd. Quite simply, he wasn't there any more. I went to collect my suitcase. Then a taxi took me home.

My apartment was in perfect order. There was no longer any trace of Jeanne. She had moved into my place a few weeks earlier, but only temporarily. Following some rather complicated business, her landlord had thrown her out, and she was looking for a new apartment. However, the suitcases she had placed in my bedroom were no longer there. I called her on her mobile, but all I got was her voicemail. I wondered where she could be. I called her mother. On the telephone, she seemed very embarrassed to be talking to me. I didn't understand why. I began to get worried. I decided to wait for news from her. Calmly. It was all I could do. I made myself a coffee. I read the few letters I had received during my absence. At one point, I got up from my desk and went into the bedroom. The last time I saw her, she was still sleeping in that unmade bed. That was four days earlier. I stirred the ashes of her body with the cold of her absence. And suddenly I thought again of that terrible image: myself, turning round, and seeing that the car is no longer there.

She called me a little later that afternoon. She was in a taxi and was on her way to her new apartment: she had found it in four days, a miracle. She absolutely insisted that I meet her there. Her excitement was at fever pitch. She gave me the address and, a moment later, I was in a taxi with a smile on my lips. It was quite a sombre street, near Censier. On the telephone, she had explained to me that the entrance was through a large, paved courtyard. The door was at the far end of the little cul-de-sac. It was a sort of loft on two floors. I rang, the entryphone crackled slightly, she told me to come in, the door was open, she was upstairs, in the middle of 'doing something'. So I went in. The sitting room was completely empty. Everything needed redoing. It was just like her to have chosen this type of apartment. I headed up the little staircase. I called to her. I went into the first room. The bedroom. She wasn't there. I heard her voice. I turned round: she was now in front of me, an apparition, with her ladybird smile. I didn't have time to say anything. She took my hand, and we went back down into the big sitting room. She stretched me out on the floor. She undressed in front of me. And we spent the rest of the afternoon making love, at least I think so.

I didn't have any news of Martin for several months. In August 2004, I received a book entitled *The Fascination of Evil* in the post. The author's name didn't mean anything to me. However, intrigued by the title, I flicked through it distractedly: it was dedicated in black ink, in minuscule, almost illegible handwriting. It took me some time to decipher it: *Since you can keep a secret. Best wishes, Martin.* I was unpleasantly surprised. Martin had recounted our trip to Egypt. He hadn't wasted any time. But why had he published it under a pseudonym? It seemed to me that this was a bad sign. And if he had chosen to hide behind a mask, why was he confiding that to me? Swiftly scanning the pages of the book, I spotted Lamia's name several times. Then mine. Yes, it was true: he had turned our trip into a short novel. The bastard. At last I was about to understand what had happened six months earlier. My throat was tight. To be completely frank, I was rather worried. But I didn't yet have the least idea of all that was going to happen because of this book.

I started reading it immediately. The story began on the morning of the departure for Egypt. The narrator gets up at dawn to take the taxi that's going to carry him off to Roissy; nothing very interesting. How can you start a novel like that? After a rather long digression about Sharm el-Sheikh, the two characters disembark at their destination, Cairo. It was a realist novel, very contemporary, throwing down crazy gauntlets to modernity, without any poetic detour or real writing—exactly what I didn't like in literature. All of the first part was more or less faithful to what had really happened: the arrival at the hotel, the first evenings, the events, the discussions about the absence of sex and about Islam. But at a given point, Martin veers away from reality; in any event, the reality I'd perceived. In the middle of the book, he writes a long parenthesis in which he recounts his meeting with Lamia, ten years earlier, in Lausanne. In the novel, the kiss isn't enough, they go as far as sleeping together. The young Moroccan girl's two brothers realise this and smash his face up; Martin is in hospital for two weeks. After that, Lamia doesn't want to see him again and, the following year, she moves to Paris. It's at that point that the character's wanderings start. And his contempt with regard to Islam.

Ten years later, by pure chance, he finds her again during his stay in Cairo. He discovers to his terror that his love for her is intact. She hasn't recognised him. He attempts clumsily to seduce her, but she ignores him completely. On the other hand, she seems less indifferent to another person; the one who bears my name. Next, he recounts his night in the brothel, that improbable story he'd told me and which, in certain respects, was a perfect indication of what was going to happen in my room at the Marriott. What's more, as I read the book, I wondered if I hadn't been manipulated right to the end: that is, right up to the punch I'd given him. Basically, I had taken Lamia up to my room, exactly as he'd asked me to do. Then I'd hit him, unwittingly following the script he'd devised himself a little earlier that evening. He himself said he'd returned to that bar, had intended to rape the girl with the green eyes before he got his face smashed up by a guy. That's the line he'd spun me a littler earlier that evening. Yes, I wondered if he had planned to replay the scene of his first humiliation and, if so, I had executed my role with overwhelming naivety. In any case, that was what his novel suggested.

I closed the book again, not entirely sure what to think. I had an unpleasant feeling. I didn't care at all for the way he'd described me personally, but in the end that was unimportant. As I saw it, the account had nothing to do with reality, but that was his right, he was a writer. After thinking about it quite a lot, it was more his words about Islam that made me feel uncomfortable. They seemed to me to be defamatory and insulting, and were such a long way from the attraction that I personally felt for all these countries. I now understood why he had used a pseudonym. These weren't real arguments, but rather a succession of prejudices on the subject, to my mind quite representative of the mindset that an average Westerner might have developed over the last few months, following international news events.

At the end of the novel, Martin went off into a sort of delirium: he described the conflict to come between the western and Muslim civilisations. He talked of the new Jewish emigration to the United States encouraged by the increasing number of anti-Semitic acts in Europe. In fact he reiterated the thesis put forward by several philosophers, stating that suspicion with regard to the Jews had found a new credibility through the Palestinian cause. True, the burning down of synagogues, the profanation of cemeteries and obscene inscriptions were generally condemned, but paradoxically they received a positive translation: after all, this violence, of Arab-Muslim origin, was a desperate reaction to their status as victims. Soon, he wrote, even terrorist acts against Europe, although not losing any of the horror they aroused, would be perceived as an understandable response to the humiliation of Muslims all over the world: first, one must take issue with oneself. On these fine sentiments attacks would flourish in Berlin, in London, but above all in Paris. The most comfortably-off Europeans would leave to live in the United States, the last more-or-less secure bastion of Western culture, and we would witness a new wave of religious migration. This time it would not be persecution by the Catholics, but virtual persecution by the Muslims that would explain these departures. And little by little, Europe would become Muslim. According to him, the European Western system quite simply had no chance.

The scandal erupted at the beginning of September. Several articles had already accused the book of rampant Islamophobia. A few days after it came out, different Muslim organisations demanded it be withdrawn from bookshops. A few voices were heard speaking up limply on behalf of freedom of expression, but the main interest was concentrated on the author's identity. Who was he? I don't know how the journalists learnt that the signature was a pseudonym. For a time people talked about Sollers, which wasn't possible, since Sollers had style and—according to *Le Monde*—would never have written 'such a bad novel'. People also mentioned Houellebecq, but here again, the rumour was improbable. It was better to search among the less important authors. Several Muslim associations returned to the Houellebecq case, regretting that he hadn't been found guilty at the time of his trial, since it was plain to see that his legal victory had opened the door to this kind of hate-filled pamphlet. All these discussions made me laugh softly. And I had the impression that nobody would ever flush out Martin.

However, his name emerged in *Le Parisien*. According to several close friends of the editor, Martin Millet was the author of *The Fascination of Evil*: that was what you were able to read, on the 23rd September, in an article entitled: "A Novel in Search of an Author". *Le Figaro* questioned him about it the following day, but to my surprise Martin forcibly denied the rumour. He even went as far as condemning the novel himself. He would never have written that book, which he considered often ambiguous, sometimes worrying, and always bad, tragically bad. His response was admirable. For the firmness and spite with which he'd expressed himself had the effect of convincing those who still doubted he was responsible: in a way it was the subtlest means of unmasking him.

I remember that I then thought of Voltaire and his *Philosophical Dictionary*. The reference was a little generous, but the situation was nonetheless comparable. From 1764 onwards, Voltaire's game consisted of vehemently denying all paternity with respect to this work and at the same time denouncing it as 'diabolical', 'abominable', 'anti-Christian', 'infernal', 'the work of Satan'. In certain letters, he attributed the *Dictionary* to a certain Debu, des Buttes, Desbuttes or Dubut who, according to the case, was an old man, an apprentice priest or a young Huguenot related to a former Jesuit. In other letters, he admitted having written the non-theological articles, this time attributing the most scabrous to various authors, collaborators on the *Encyclopaedia* (Dumarsais, Boulanger), pastors from Geneva (Abauzit, Polier de Bottens), English writers (Middleton, Warburton), all dead or not living in France. This is how he became the most famous non-author in Europe.

Why was Martin playing this game? Doubtless there was a little of the pleasure of striking while concealing his hand. But it seems to me that these evasive manoeuvres could be explained above all by caution, and even fear. But the fear of what? Back then, Voltaire had settled at Ferney, a short step from the Swiss border, on his fief, which he claimed was independent of the King of France. For Martin, the situation was different. And it was moreover his Swiss identity, transposed onto that of his principal character, which drew suspicion to him. In any case, after the *Figaro* article, nobody doubted any longer that he was the author of *The Fascination of Evil*, and it was at that point that his troubles began.

Several newspapers published very short extracts and quotations out of context, thus fuelling the debate—which was enough to sentence the novel to death. Media coverage always works like a trap for literature. Here and there you could read the offending or problematic passages, thus transforming the book into a simple corpus delicti. *Le Point* put together a dossier on "The New Islamophobia" and took as its angle not the book, but Martin Millet himself. 'Should we tolerate intolerance?' a journalist in the *Nouvel Observateur* asked sagely. According to him, the freedom of expression had become a comfortable windbreak against the stench of hatred. In *Le Monde* on the 3rd October, Boubakeur wrote a long article in which Martin was directly accused of racism. The rector of the Great Mosque forgot completely that this was a 'novel'. That which was written summed up the writer's thoughts exactly, otherwise it was not written: that, in brief, was his reasoning. Several sentences in his article even let it be understood clearly that the text was an incitement to racial hatred. The following day, on the radio, Martin replied that one could fully express reservations about the positive worth of a religion without at the same time inciting people to 'racial hatred'. He reminded listeners briefly that a religion was above all a system for explaining the world and that in this respect, condemning one of them was a philosophical act that, by definition, had nothing to do with those who adhered to it. Talk of racism in his case came purely and simply from lumping the two together, and could not be done except by cretins in power and crusaders who simplified everything and were dramatically dense ... (You could sense from his voice that he was nervous and might easily slip up.) He laid a great deal of emphasis on one point: for him, Islam must learn to be criticised, rightly or wrongly, like any other religion.

In the bookshops, the book was a success, which complicated the situation even more. The author was suspected of having scribbled two or three lines against Islam with the sole intention of causing a scandal and selling his unreadable book. Another article, this time in *Libération*, signed by a guy I had already noted for his stupidity, went even further in this endeavour to confuse and denounce. It talked of the 'unacceptable behaviour of certain Westerners in poor countries' and assured readers, without having apparently read it, that *The Fascination of Evil* displayed a disdainful view of women, children, Arabs and animals, including species threatened with extinction, and that one could not help but be indignant in the face of this 'neo-colonialist stench'. Agitated, the World Islamic League, the National Federation of French Muslims, and the Ritual Association of the great mosque in Lyon took legal action against Martin Millet and his publisher for 'provocation to discrimination, hatred or violence and insult towards a group of individuals because of their membership of a specified religion, in this case Islam'. The SPA added itself to the list of plaintiffs because of ambiguous, even faintly spiteful words spoken by the main character (no doubt the author) about parrots, which is unacceptable.

Martin was invited on different TV shows to explain himself. He was asked clearly if he had written this book with the intention of creating a scandal, even obtaining a *fatwa*. Martin replied jokingly that a *fatwa* couldn't be launched against a non-Muslim and that he would therefore have to agree to convert, which he wasn't planning to do in the immediate future. He was against all forms of religion. On the show, a woman from goodness knows where explained, with tears in her eyes, that the Koran was a very beautiful book and that she couldn't understand how anyone could tolerate such repugnant accounts being added to the horror of the international situation. In the studio, the audience applauded her enthusiastically. I then thought of that sentence I'd read, a few days before in a formidable essay: *The cursed ones of the nineteenth century were cursed through shadows and silence.* Could it be that those of today are cursed through light and sound?

Fortunately, certain intellectuals took up Martin's defence. A petition circulated: it insisted on the importance of lay opinions, on the immunity of fiction and on the regressive step that would be represented by the implicit reinstatement of the crime of blasphemy. It also reminded people that one could admire a writer without following him in all his phobias. The list of examples was long. And so as not to sacrifice anything to ignorance, it quoted a few extracts from Montaigne (who regarded Mohammed as one of those "mocking individuals who bend to our stupidity in order to lure us with honeyed words") and from Pascal (who considered those passages of the Koran which were not "obscure" to be "ridiculous"). In indignation, certain associations wanted to attack these two authors, but had to abandon the idea after a spot of research; they had in fact been dead for a long time.

Dominique Noguez wrote an article denouncing the "madness of not reading". Effectively, nobody had any further doubts about what was being peddled by the few hurried journalists, too happy to be able to seize upon a real little scandal to take the trouble of thinking about the accusations they were making. Nobody had any further doubts: Martin had written a loathsome book in which Islam was odiously attacked. The text no longer had any importance. Nobody referred to it any more. It no longer existed.

Personally, I didn't like the book much, but I was forced to admit that not all the criticisms that were made of it were valid and that they doubtless bore witness, yes, to a madness of not reading that which was really written. The debate was lost in the most extreme confusion. In the din, one began to realise that a novelist could no longer tackle the very sensitive subject of Islam without taking crazy precautions. You had to handle the touchy issues with kid gloves, politely censor yourself so as not to find yourself accused of the most grotesque things. All of this heralded, in a way, the death of fiction. In other places, this would quite simply have been called: the exercise of terror.

At the end of October, quite unexpectedly, I received a call from Martin. It took me a while to recognise his voice, and at first I thought it was a joke. He seemed very anxious. He asked me how I was and explained to me, without even waiting for my response, that he was in a terrifying situation. The media atmosphere of the lynch mob had completely undermined him. In particular, he was receiving threats every day. Notably messages in Arabic on his answering machine or his email, whose meaning, even without a translator, it was easy to guess.

"It's just to frighten you," I told him, not paying too much attention to what he was telling me.

"Maybe not … "

His voice was jerky. I didn't know what to think. Was he really at any risk? I had the feeling he was exaggerating. After all, his novel wasn't sufficiently important to place him in physical danger. He seemed to think the opposite. For several days now, he had stopped going out. He was planning to go abroad soon, doubtless to Italy. To wait until the dust settled, he said. It might be a good idea. I didn't know. But until then, he was hoping for some police protection. Several times that week, someone had rung his doorbell with 'murderous insistence'. Also, insulting and threatening letters had been placed in his mailbox. The first bullet will be for me, he said. The first bullet will be for me.

I had the feeling he was exaggerating. "And it's all the more horrible since I'm not the author of this book … " Even with me, he continued his strategy of denial. I knew he was excessive by nature. And the promotion of a book often has a tendency, I also knew, to accentuate paranoid tendencies. To my mind, he had no need to worry: it was only a novel, and the violence he was feeling wasn't destined for him, it was the violence borne by the complicated question of Islam in France. "You know," I told him, "the French Muslim community has already suffered a lot with everything that's happening in the world ... " He suggested we have a drink together. He wanted to talk to me about "certain important things". I agreed, a little perplexed, all the time reproaching myself for not being sufficiently unpleasant with him. After what had happened. Because I had to be away from Paris for a few days, which wasn't true, we had to fix the meeting for four days later.

It was a Monday. The café was called L'Espérance. I reckon I was more or less on time. There was nobody left in the back room. I had no idea what he wanted to tell me, and the fact of being there, waiting for him, had something very unpleasant about it. I remembered what he had told me about possible police security, and I imagined him entering L'Espérance with two bodyguards. It would have looked very Salman Rushdie. But he didn't come. While I waited, I remember, I was rereading *The Odyssey*. What's more, I had time to read three Cantos. It didn't surprise me about him. I didn't have his number. I couldn't do anything but wait. But after a while I nevertheless went home, rather furious.

Until the following day, I had no news of him. I remembered his sudden disappearance in Cairo, and told myself that he must do this regularly. The strange thing, now I think back, is the extent to which I suspected nothing. I had been so irrationally anxious in Cairo, during his bogus disappearance, succumbing immediately to what Lamia had rightly called 'the fascination of evil', but his absence from L'Espérance had aroused no more than powerless anger in me.

It wasn't until Tuesday evening that I realised what had

happened. I was working when my publisher called. There was something unusual about his voice. In general, even when he told me bad news I had the feeling it was good news: he was one of those people who always present things in an excessively positive way, to the point of completely confusing you and making you doubt the very worth of what is being said. Now, however, the timbre of his voice was clear as an announcement for a dramatic play. Something had happened. Martin's body had been discovered. Apparently, he had been murdered two days previously. In his apartment. This seemed impossible to me. Unreal. What! All he'd done was write a book, nothing more … To convince myself, I went and bought the paper. The article in *Le Figaro* explained that someone had shot a bullet into his head. A feeling of horror overtook me. A suspect had been arrested: one Islamic extremist among others, who confessed his crime a few days later, without awkwardness, specifying that French justice had demonstrated more than once that it did not condemn Islamophobic works and that from now on people must expect another, more intransigent justice, handed down in an autonomous, direct way. The majority of Muslim associations condemned this act as well as this declaration. In the press, people started talking about the passages in the Koran inciting the extermination of infidels, and notably *Suras* V, IX and XLVII, of which the following is an extract: *When you encounter unbelievers, strike them on the back of the neck until you have killed them.*

Martin was buried ten days later in Montparnasse Cemetery. It was cold that day. You could already feel the winter coming on. As well as that other winter, the premonition of which had already given me violent shivers. People compared the situation with that of Rushdie. In 1988, after the publication of *The Satanic Verses*, Ayatollah Khomeini had sentenced that author to death for blasphemy and had sent hired killers after him. The sentence had finally been lifted. For more than ten years, Rushdie had lived under close protection in England, then in New York. I went to Martin's funeral. He hadn't been so lucky. The first bullet had been for him.

I remembered what Kundera had written about that writer. This situation was unique in history and derived from a fundamental confrontation between several eras: "Through his origins, Rushdie belongs to Muslim society which, to a large extent, is still living in the age before modern times. He wrote his book in Europe, in the era of modern times or, more exactly, at the end of that era." In the same way, those who strive today to stifle creative freedom with their good feelings, and who are unfortunately listened to with increasing frequency, are brought back by their preoccupations to the obscurantism that existed before the triumph of reason. For Kundera, the novel is by its very essence the work of Europe. Once again, when he says 'European novel', he isn't talking about what has been created in Europe by Europeans, but about what belongs in literary terms to a story that began at the dawn of modern times in Europe. Now, he considers that this European art is by definition incompatible with all religious thinking: for it is by its essence a kind of profanation. The novel is something that makes whatever it touches ungraspable and which thus derives from man's moral ambiguity and from the fundamental relativity of things. Those who think they possess the truth and will not accept contradiction are therefore directly threatened by the art of the novel. So they have a cruel interest in destroying it. With Rushdie, it is the art of the novel as such that the Ayatollah wanted to kill. With Martin Millet, it's fiction itself that was the target. And it is rather surprising to note that Europe has so much difficulty defending the most European of arts, that is to say in defending its own culture. We content ourselves with a small petition, and then go home. Cowardly alms-giving: yes, we donate a couple of coins and then carry on our way. And then fear comes.

That day, there was practically nobody in Montparnasse Cemetery. Europe was not excessively moved by the fact that its most characteristic art had just been sentenced to death. The mood was disastrous. People shook hands. Shivered. Everybody spat out smoke as they breathed out. They wanted to forget and move on to something else. Yes, the mood was disastrous because for all of us, I think, it conjured up those funeral pyres lit by generations of morons and which had made life hard for those who today make up the foundations of our culture. Where have the powerful men of that same era gone, men like the Cardinal du Bellay, Cardinal Odet, François I, who ensured that hunted writers were protected? "But is Europe still Europe? That is to say, the society of the novel? In other words: is it still in the era of modern times? Is it not already entering another era which doesn't yet have a name, and for which its arts no longer have much importance?" Those, among others, were the questions I asked myself as I left Montparnasse Cemetery.

PS: Is there any point in my stipulating that I entirely refute the rumours that spread in the months that followed, claiming that I was the true author of *The Fascination of Evil*? I remind all those who peddle these insinuations that Martin Millet implicitly recognised that he had signed that book and that I would not have amused myself by leaving indications in the text enabling him to be wrongly identified. I never wished Martin Millet any ill, and I am not an assassin.

FLORIAN ZELLER

Lovers or something like it

Translated by
Sue Dyson

When disaffected young Parisian Tristan meets pretty, fragile Amelie, he is thrown off guard by his feelings for her. He had sworn to stay single forever, loving and leaving a trail of heart-broken women in his wake. He hasn't done anything to deserve falling in love: why him and why Amelie? Is she really so special? Tristan is torn between tenderness and desire, and as their relationship grows ever more complex, he finds it impossible to avoid betrayal.

Lovers or something like it is an intelligent and sensitive portrayal of the doubts and desires of a new generation, suffering from the agony of indecision and too many choices to feel true contentment.

"Florian Zeller has a talent that can be frightening ... each page of the novel contains something astonishing ... Zeller is disarming. More than promising, he is bursting with talent."
AURELIE SARROT *Metro*

ISBN 1-901285-52-9 · 168pp · £8.99

SIMON LIBERATI

Anthology of Apparitions

Translated by
Paul Buck & Catherine Petit

Claude is a fallen angel from the hedonistic
1970's nightclubbing scene in Paris and St
Tropez. As *Anthology of Apparitions* begins, he
is in his forties, destroyed by the mystery of
his sister's disappearance—he sits in a cafe
drinking and day-dreaming. Only the ghostly
appearances from his past make life tolerable.
Claude is haunted by memories and visions
of 1976, when he was sixteen and his sister
Marina only a child. Together they belonged
to the world of wild young things living on the
edge, but when Marina started to lose her way,
Claude did nothing to save her.

"*Anthology of Apparitions* is a valuable and at times
tender examination of an unenviable, alien soul."
SIMON BAKER *New Statesman*

ISBN 1-901285-58-8 · 180pp · £8.99